Tell

Me

Why

by

Ruth O'Neill

www.publishnation.co.uk

Other works by the author:

Sunshine & Tears, a novel, published 2015

Befriended, a novel, published 2018

To Annie

Best Wishes

Ruth o'Neill

xxx

For Rachel

CONTENTS

Chapter One

The Rescue

"Please, bring my sister back alive!"

"I'll do my best."

Kevin attached the air-line breathing apparatus to his back; a lifeline was attached to his harness, running back to a point outside the confined space. He tied a wristlet around his waist, hoping it would pull Lauren to safety.

Jacob looked on as the rescue team prepared themselves. He thought it was taking too long, but as excruciating as the situation was, he knew that for the rescue attempt to be successful the men would have to put their safety first. Recovering from the desperate rhythm of his shallow breathing, all he could do now was wait.

Once again, he called out to Kevin who was about to climb into the crawl space. "Please, bring Lauren back!"

Kevin didn't reply this time; he just nodded at Jacob. In his line of work, he knew not to make promises he might not be able to keep.

His crewmember Eddie positioned himself next to the entrance, both so he could keep watch and so he could communicate with Kevin. "Good luck, mate," he whispered.

Kevin signalled a thumbs-up before starting to edge his way into the small cavernous hole, trying not to think of how small it was as he inched his way along the ill-lit tunnel; the headlight attached to his helmet wasn't giving him any clear vision. A mild brush of claustrophobia came and went, Kevin having pushed the fear away before it could even try to settle in his brain; he knew he couldn't give into that type of thinking, not when there was a life at stake.

Eddie had relayed all the information he'd collected from Jacob, and by his calculations he estimated there to be another twenty minutes before he would reach Lauren – twenty minutes she simply might not have.

Trying not to think about that, Kevin hummed his favourite tune; he did this every time he went on a rescue attempt as it helped him – usually – keep a clear head. The sound coming from inside his filter mask, however, wasn't so much a hum but a muffled moan.

Looking down at his gloves, he saw they were black. He put his hand to his nose, flinching; he'd smelled this odour before, and he knew it wasn't a good sign. He crawled along faster on his elbows and knees, his shoulders becoming stuck every so often and forcing him to manoeuvre his body sideways in order to free himself. The equipment he was carrying made it all the more difficult, but still he soldiered on.

After a while he began to make good headway, and as he turned a corner he could see the outline of a body ahead of him. His energy seemed to be evaporating, but five more moves and Kevin thought he could reach her. He snatched away his filter mask, pushing himself to move quicker. He was within touching distance now. He crawled towards her slowly, not wanting to frighten the poor woman.

"Lauren, my name is Kevin," he said gently. "I'm here to get you out."

Kevin could just about hear Lauren's laboured breathing, and removing his gloves, he picked her arm up to feel for a pulse. It was there, but it was weak. He navigated the water bottle out from the small bag fastened to his leg, then considered how to give it to her. After a moment, he decided to roll onto his side, so his face could touch hers. Then, raising his left arm, he guided the water bottle nozzle over to Lauren's dry, cracked lips.

"Lauren, you need to sip some water. Can you open your mouth for me?" No response. Kevin gently picked up her hand. "Lauren, squeeze my hand if you can hear me." Kevin waited. A slight tweak. At least there was a response. At least there was something.

Her eyes flickered. Slowly, they opened.

"You need to drink some water, love," Kevin said as he lifted up the bottle. Lauren's mouth parted and Kevin let a slow flow of drips meet her lips. Her body jerked as she swallowed. She coughed, her face contorted in pain.

"Slowly, Lauren, slowly," Kevin said softly. "Now, I need you to listen to me while I explain what's going to happen. I'm going to tie a wristlet – a cloth strap – around your ankle, quite tightly. Then, once it's looped around your foot I'm going to attach it to a rope and I'm going to pull you along. Lauren, it will tighten around your foot, but don't be alarmed – it's meant to do that. First I'm going to put an air-line oxygen mask over your nose and mouth so you can breathe more easily. Will that be okay, Lauren?"

Lauren liked the sound of this voice. It was calm and gave her hope, the dim light surrounding her giving her an unexpected surge of energy. When her brother had left her she'd just wanted him to live, not much caring what happened to her; she'd had enough of Max destroying her, had had enough of everything. But now, listening to this man, she wanted to live too.

She looked up into his eyes and nodded. For the first time in a long while, she felt safe. She didn't resist the rubber mask as it covered her nose and mouth – after taking a few deep breaths, it felt good to be able to breathe again.

"Okay," said the man, "what I need you to do now is to slowly turn yourself around. I need you to rotate your body so that your feet are facing me. Can you do this, Lauren?"

Lauren nodded as she began shuffling her body onto her side. She was so weak… how was she going to do this? As she rolled back to her starting position her eyes locked on Kevin's, revealing her desperation.

"Take your time, Lauren." Kevin tried to relax her as best he could, but having already used at least twenty-five minutes' worth of oxygen, he was concerned they might run out. It was going to take much longer to get back than he'd thought – but he'd worry about that later.

Slowly, Lauren steered her body into the opposite direction, her legs buckling up into a crouching position. Then, shuffling along on her bottom, she guided herself with her hands. She'd forgotten about the dry, dusty dirt floor until tiny particles of earth scooted up in front of her like a fountain, entering her eyes and causing her to blink furiously to remove the grit. She'd only got halfway, and she was exhausted. She took a deep breath, her lungs welcoming the extra oxygen. She hadn't spoken one word to Kevin yet. She removed the mask.

"Is Jacob okay?" Her voice came out in a low rasp, as if her vocal chords had been paralysed.

"He's safe and well, waiting for you," replied Kevin.

Lauren smiled before replacing the mask – she couldn't do without it just yet. Kevin's reply had given her the motivation she needed to carry on, and in one big thrust she threw herself full circle, scraping her head against the rough jagged roof of the crawl space. She winced as she felt the liquid run down her face.

Kevin fastened the wristlet around her ankle, aware that she had a large cut above her forehead. He wouldn't be able to tend to her injury in here – he just had to hope the bleeding would ease. When he pulled the wristlet tight, Lauren's foot jerked upwards.

"Sorry, but it has to be tight, Lauren," he told her gently. "As I pull you along, if you can try and shift your body at the same time, it will put less strain on your ankle."

Lauren waved her hand, signalling that she understood.

"Now, after the count of three, shift. One, two, three – shift!" Kevin pulled the wristlet at the same time as he pushed himself forward, but there was no shift from Lauren, just dead weight.

"Let's try again. One, two, three – shift!"

There was a slight movement from Lauren this time but they didn't get very far.

"Right, Lauren, I might have to drag you. I'm sorry, but it might be painful."

Lauren waved her hand again, indicating it was okay; the amount of pain she'd already endured wouldn't see her complaining now. A raging headache was brewing inside her head, but she had to concentrate. Her focus was Jacob now – not Max. Just thinking of his name made her skin crawl.

The only things that kept her going during her incarceration were thoughts of Jacob and her mother, her only family. And she was going to think of them again now to get her through the pain barrier – to get her to freedom. Her body was about to give up but she was going to do her damn hardest not to let it. She felt a hard tug on her ankle as she moved with a sudden jolt.

"One, two, three – shift!" She could hear Kevin's words as he kept on repeating them.

After taking another big, deep breath, the oxygen flowed freely to her lungs. With this added boost, this time she managed to push her bottom to the floor and propel her body forward with her hands. At the same time Kevin pulled hard on the wristlet, scooting her along the ground.

"That's good, Lauren!" shouted Kevin. "Now we just need to keep this up!"

We just need to keep this up, she thought. *But what if she couldn't?*

Suddenly, it was like she was coming to her senses, finally realising where she was – stuffed in what was essentially a coffin, with little air and very little light. All she could see was a faint glow that beamed upwards from Kevin's headlight, and suddenly she felt trapped. It was as if time was slowing down. The tug on her foot made her scream; she'd forgotten to keep in unison with Kevin. The wristlet seared into her skin.

Kevin stopped. "Are you okay, Lauren?"

She removed the oxygen mask, dragging her hands across her cheeks and leaving behind streaks of dirt and congealed blood. "I don't know if I can carry on," she murmured.

Kevin looked back over his shoulder. Lauren didn't look good. "Stay strong," he told her. "It's not much further, I promise." Kevin knew there were at least another fifteen minutes to go until they reached safety – and that was only if they could continue to move along simultaneously –but Lauren didn't need to know that. "Put the mask back on, Lauren," he said, "you need to regulate your breathing. Can you do that for me?"

Lauren couldn't hide the exhaustion and depletion her body felt. She was being pushed to the limits and her emotional resilience was in tatters. She wanted to scream, to curl up in a ball and simply drift to sleep.

She threw the oxygen mask at Kevin – it landed only a stone's throw away from her – and then she drew her knees up, ripping the cloth strap from her bleeding, swollen ankle. Her racing heart wasn't being kind to her but it was enough for her to want to give up. She felt detached. Numb. Alone.

For a few seconds her brain vibrated quickly, causing a low-pitched humming sound in her ears, and as she looked up, fuzzy, snow-like fission darted everywhere.

An urgent feeling of needing to escape overtook her body. If she didn't, she was sure she would faint. Shaking, sweating, and twitching, she knew she needed to move. If she stayed still any longer she wasn't going to make it.

"I can't breathe! I can't do this!" she shrieked.

She started shaking then, feeling cold and hot at the same time. She felt her hair standing on end as she constantly heard nails scraping on a chalkboard. She sobbed uncontrollably, her whole body racked with pain.

She couldn't do this. She wasn't going to make it. Her body was – finally, and with a great amount of relief – giving up on her.

With this thought she closed her eyes, a single tear running down her cheek and coming to a stop just above her dry, cracked lips.

"Lauren?" Kevin asked as he stared at her deathly pale face, her closed eyes, "Lauren? No... don't do this to me... Lauren!"

Chapter Two

Two years ago

Lauren zipped up the vibrant red suitcase and glanced at her watch – one hour until she needed to set off. Taking the stairs two at a time, she popped into her lounge, smiling as she looked into the ornate mirror. Ringlets of brown hair circled her face. Large hazel eyes adorned with bronze eye shadow and a thick coat of extreme black mascara stared back at her. Her pouty lips were a bright flaming red – not exactly a subtle look for this time of day, but she always liked to make a statement.

Sitting on the brown leather armchair, she turned on her phone to find three text messages – the first one from Chloe. *See you soon Hun. Chloe xx.*

Lauren smiled as she thought of her friend. The first day they'd met, there had been an instant connection. Both had sat there, nervously waiting to be interviewed for a job at Foster's Menswear. Short skirts and low-cut tops had been both of their strategies to gain employment – and it worked. They'd celebrated together that day fifteen years ago and had been friends ever since.

Chloe was now in a relationship with Aaron, and Lauren had to admit, she felt envious; she wanted to be settled down and in love too. That hadn't happened for her – yet – but she hoped this weekend might change that.

Don't forget Sambuca – text number two was from Kate. Kate was the fun one of the group. Life had dealt her a bad hand, suffering from rheumatoid arthritis for years, but it didn't stop her from enjoying herself. Kate had saved up her medication especially for this weekend; she wasn't going to let anything spoil her chance at fun. Kate was thirty-five, divorced, and living with her mother. She wasn't looking for anyone else to share her life with – she was happy enough to be single again after living through eight tumultuous years of marriage.

The third text read, *What are you wearing? Holly x.* Holly was the more serious one, always needing to keep everything under control. Lauren always thought it was nice to have someone she could rely on if things ended up messy; Holly was always ready to pick you up, brush you off, and get you back on the right track. Her planning of the weekend had been like a military regime. *If any of us were about to break it,* Lauren thought, *she'd be the one to rein us all back in.*

That left Lucy. Lucy was the quiet one – until alcohol was consumed. Then she was outgoing, flirty, funny, and free of all inhibitions.

This was their friendship group. They didn't always see each other on a regular basis, but they were forever arranging trips away.

This particular trip was a soul weekend at Butlin's holiday park, Minehead, situated in Somerset. A two-night stay in a six-berth caravan had looked inviting, and Lauren was excited to spend time with the girls. It would be a laugh if nothing else.

All the girls lived within a five-mile radius of each other in Salford, Greater Manchester. Lauren loved Salford Quays because of its modern cultural and entertainment community, which showed off sparkling architecture and waterside dining. They'd all enjoyed many drunken nights there, dancing the night away and ignoring the beautiful location they lived in.

Lauren quickly replied to all three texts, then decided to make a quick FaceTime video call to her mother before setting off. This always made her laugh – her mother would sit poker straight and repeat, "Can you see me, Lauren? I can see you in the small picture." She'd often say, "The only drawback about FaceTime is you're reachable wherever you are, even if you don't want to be."

"Hello, Mum." The connection was quick.

"Is that you, Lauren?"

"Mum, take the phone away from your ear. Look at the screen."

"Oh, there you are. You look nice. Where you off to?"

"Away for the weekend with the girls, remember? I told you last week."

"Oh yes, so you did. So you won't be popping around for Sunday lunch this weekend?"

"No, not this weekend."

"Weather isn't going to be very good – I hope you've packed some warm clothes."

Lauren stared at her mother on the screen. She was a glamorous woman, with the kindest eyes she'd ever seen, her beautiful long hair always pinned up in a bun. Her mother was not only loved by those around her, but by everyone she met; her compassionate, caring nature just drew strangers to her.

"Lauren, can you hear me? Beryl from next door said, Nancy, you need to gather all those wet leaves up off your grass, otherwise they will destroy it. I'm not going out in this cold weather to pick up leaves, I told her. Mr Graham, from the village, volunteered to come round to pick them up. What a kind soul he is. I don't think Beryl liked *that* very much."

"Yes, I can hear you, Mum. Don't worry about the leaves; I'll pick them up next weekend. Mum, I need to go now. I just wanted to check you're okay."

"I'm fine, Lauren. Goodbye, and have a lovely time."

"Bye, Mum. Love you," she said, but the screen had already closed. Lauren smiled as she pictured her mother continuously stabbing her finger at the end call icon.

Tossing her phone into her handbag, she grabbed her case and locked the door on her way out.

Lauren threw the suitcase into the boot of Clara, her small A1 Mercedes. Lauren had a name for all her possessions. She liked it that way; it meant she was in control. The other girls, however, thought she was mad. She had no one else in her life, and making up names for different objects at home made her think she had her own family, in a way. At thirty-two years old, time was beginning to slip away from her. She'd always dreamed of having a husband, a house, and children by the time she reached her thirties, but none of those things had happened. Yes, she had her own rented flat with a small garden, but what she really wanted was her own family. She kept telling herself not to worry about it. There were plenty of thirty-somethings out there in the big wide world in her exact position. At least she had the children she supported at school; Lauren loved her job as a teaching assistant at Salford Primary. Her ten years there had all been happy ones.

Lauren grinned as she slammed the boot shut, and after climbing into Clara she placed her handbag down on the passenger seat, excited to be setting off. Her excitement soon started to wane, however, when she saw how many cars were on the roads – the thirty-minute drive to Chloe's soon turning into an hour's drive. Early Friday afternoon traffic had not been kind to her.

When she finally got there Chloe was standing on the doorstep to greet her, pointing at her gold Rolex watch. "What time do you call this?" Chloe asked as she kissed Lauren on the cheek.

"Bloody traffic – not my fault." Lauren managed a half-smile.

"Not to worry. We're all ready to leave anyway."

"Leave? I need wine before we leave!" Lauren pushed past Chloe, leaving her suitcase on the drive as she greeted each of her friends with a kiss on the cheek. "Hi, girls!"

"You can have wine in the car; at this rate we'll be lucky if we get there before dark!" Chloe shouted as she loaded up the car. Salford was four hours away from Minehead, and Chloe was clearly eager to get on the road.

"Okay, okay. Let's get going, then. The quicker we get there, the quicker the party will begin!" huffed Lauren.

All five girls piled into Chloe's four-by-four, Lauren choosing to sit in the middle of the back seat, with Lucy to her right and Holly to her left. Kate sat in the passenger seat in the front so she'd have more room for her arthritic feet. Her swollen arm was in a sling – a flare-up she'd been expecting due to the medication she'd chosen not to take. Once they'd set foot in the caravan and she'd taken the meds, the swelling would be gone within the hour.

Once Lauren had poured out the wine for the non-drivers, she shouted, "Cheers, girls, and here's to a great weekend!" She raised her glass, and Holly, Kate, and Lucy shouted 'cheers' in unison.

The four-hour drive passed quickly; by the time they got there three empty wine bottles lay at Lauren's feet, the girls all in high spirits.

As they approached the entrance to Butlin's, they spied parties of people in fancy dress. A man wearing a mankini that left nothing to the imagination was being cheered by passers-by, and Kate leant over and sounded the horn. Chloe opened the window to send out a wolf-whistle. The girls laughed, sensing the carnival atmosphere.

As Chloe parked up close to reception, Lucy volunteered to go and book them all in. Within a few minutes she came out with a map and the keys to caravan number seventy-six.

The girls were laughing and joking, but Lauren was more concerned with what was going on outside the car; she'd noticed what appeared to be the shadow of a man lurking in the trees near the reception, and though she couldn't see his face, she had the creepiest sensation that he was staring directly at them.

Just then Chloe asked her if she was okay, and Lauren turned to reply. When she looked back at the trees a second or so later, the shadow was gone.

Lauren shook her head, smiling to herself. It must have been the wine getting to her.

As they started driving again they looked around at their surroundings, the manicured grounds and gardens looking like a maze.

"Whoever designed the layout of this place was seriously deluded," Lucy squealed as she studied the map. "The numbers of the caravans don't correspond in any way."

"Let me see that." Holly snatched the paper from Lucy.

Holly was the first to work out the puzzle: the numbers were set out in diagonal rows. The other girls couldn't be bothered to listen to her wittering on about how to solve a mathematic enigma, but after they'd driven in circles for fifteen minutes they were grateful when she pointed to their caravan.

As the sun descended below the horizon, the white, shiny, pre-painted aluminium panels of the caravan gleamed. Alongside it was a wooden table with benches. A wire fence bordering their pitch unveiled woodland plants, making the domain look more like a nature reserve – an idyllic setting in which to spend the weekend.

Inside, beige floral curtains matched the beige floral carpet. Comfortable seating circled the dining room, and wooden chairs were set around a small table, enough for everyone to have a place to eat. A small kitchenette area would only be used for an unhealthy fry up in the mornings, to help cure their hangovers. There were three bedrooms but only one with an en-suite. Kate gave a dynamic speech as to why she should have it, and no one could refuse her. She would share the large double bed with Holly. That left two rooms to be nabbed, one with two single beds, the other a small space with a single bed. Lucy talked Chloe and Lauren round to the idea of her having the single room, as she snored. This they knew all too well; on several occasions they'd had to listen to Lucy sounding like a beached whale at night. With the sleeping arrangements agreed on, Lucy opened the Prosecco Chloe had been waiting for.

"This is a little disheartening," said Holly, eyeing the interior.

"What is?" asked Chloe.

"This," Holly said, pointing her finger around the caravan, "it's pretty basic."

"You booked it," mumbled Kate.

"What did you expect for the money?" asked Lauren before adding, "Well, I think it's cosy. At least everything's clean."

Lucy handed a glass of fizz to everyone.

"Holly, don't worry about it. Here's to a good night!" beamed Lucy as she raised her glass.

"Right. We need a plan," said Holly after she'd taken a sip of her drink.

"A plan," the girls echoed together, laughing loudly.

"You may well jest, you lot, but this is a big place, and we don't know the vicinity yet." Holly shrugged her shoulders.

"What is the plan then, Holly?" Chloe said smugly. "Hit us, Holly, one more time!" she sang loudly, doing her best Britney Spears.

"We all stick together, okay?" Holly asked the girls. "At no time are we to be separated. If you need the loo, always go in twos, understood?"

"Yes, Holly," the girls replied in unison, saluting for good measure.

Rolling her eyes, Holly trundled off to the bedroom.

"We're joking, Holly. Come back here!" Kate shouted.

Holly came running in, a half-smile on her face. "Got you!"

Laughing, Kate threw a cushion at her. It landed straight in her face.

"Come on – group hug!" Lauren motioned her arms into a circle as the girls joined her. This was their infamous habit.

It wasn't long before the girls had unpacked, and soon they were preparing – rather noisily – for their night out.

Tonight's dress theme was black and white. Lauren chose black-and-white jeans, a black halterneck top, and a black Afro wig. Holly, the more reserved of the group, decided on a black-and-white mid-length dress with white knee-high boots. Her shiny black hair – which was the envy of all the other girls – fell to her shoulders in lovely soft waves. Kate was dressed in black leather trousers and a plain white T-shirt, a black-and-white trilby adding the finishing touch. Lucy opted for black jeans with a white off-the-shoulder blouse and black bow tie. Chloe, determined to out-do all the others, wore a black-and-white jumpsuit. Their group name tonight was 'The Two-tone Five'.

After a few more drinks – by which point they were all feeling more than a little tipsy and pretty excited – they made their way to the venue, looking forward to seeing the reggae band.

Lauren felt happily merry as she walked with her friends, though underneath the drunken contentment there was something else, something that made her keep checking the area as she went. She kept thinking back to the shadow she'd seen in the trees when they'd arrived, at how she was sure the man – whoever he was – was staring at the car. Just the memory of it made her shudder. After all, who would be skulking around in the shadows in Butlin's of all places? A strange person, that was for sure.

"You okay?" asked Chloe, frowning. "You look worried, and we're meant to be having fun!"

"Oh, I'm fine," Lauren replied, smiling at her friend. "In fact, I'm great! Let's get this show on the road, shall we?"

By the time they got there the place was already packed to capacity with revellers, and as soon as Lauren was surrounded by all the noise and the lights, she completely forgot about the man lurking in the trees. Chloe and Lauren were nominated to collect the drinks, and they politely barged their way toward the crowded bar. Some of the punters smiled, while others mouthed the odd explicit word, unhappy at being jostled. It was a free-for-all. Lauren ordered double gin and tonics – she didn't fancy having to fight her way back to the bar again anytime soon.

"I didn't want a gin and tonic; a soft drink would've done me," complained Holly as they fought their way back through the crowd.

"Well, you've got this now, so just drink it – unless you want to fight your way back to the bar." Lauren felt slightly annoyed. Holly was getting on her nerves; she wished she'd lighten up a bit.

Once the band started playing the crowd moved like crazy, and wanting to join in the fun, the girls started dancing. Holly's arms flailed everywhere; she looked like a windmill as she came at Lauren. At least she finally seemed to be enjoying herself.

The band was energetic and charismatic, interacting with the crowd between songs (they were playing covers of old reggae tunes). Picking out Holly, the lead singer commented on her knee-high boots. "Are those boots made for walking, or dancing?" he asked, causing Holly to scream out, "Dancing!" as she did a twirl. The alcohol had gone straight to her head. Dancing and singing along to the band, Kate felt like a new woman. Now that her steroids had been washed down with alcohol she was pain-free, and she danced with a huge smile on her face.

Lucy was dancing with an older guy; he held her hand as he twirled her around like a professional ice skater. His friends clapped and cheered them on.

The music was so loud that Lauren couldn't hear anyone's conversation, so although she needed the loo she didn't think to bother with Holly's two-at-a-time plan – if she were to ask one of her friends to go with her they wouldn't be able to hear what she was saying anyway. So, instead, she headed towards the bright pink neon light flashing the words 'ladies' toilets' on her own.

As she grappled her way through the crowd and struggled to push past partygoers Lauren became more and more impatient, and having her ass grabbed twice by leering men made her push through the throng even faster. As she looked around, she couldn't see any talent. No muscly hunks on show, and no forty-year-olds – this wasn't going to be the place to meet her dream man after all.

Finally she made it, feeling like she'd been pulled through a hedge backwards. One look in the mirror confirmed that. Her make-up was melting off and her black Afro wig was perched precariously on one side of her head. She laughed as she removed it, fluffing her own hair up to give it some volume. That was better; she looked half decent again. Stuffing the wig into her satchel bag, she ran into the toilet cubicle. Sensing germs everywhere, she carefully placed squares of toilet roll around the seat and then squirted hand sanitiser onto her palms.

After ten minutes spent in the toilets she was ready to embark on the tussle to return to her friends, though as she'd lost all sense of direction she aimed to just walk straight ahead. The crowd had thinned out and she realised the band had stopped playing, too. She looked at her watch – eleven thirty. That was early for the band to finish. Surely there must be other things going on? Once she'd reunited with her friends, she'd make them explore.

But first she had to find them.

Lauren was sure she'd passed the rainbow-covered glitter ball that hung unsteadily from the roof beam more than once, and as she looked around the room her heart raced and her breathing quickened. As she walked all around the venue, scouring for any sign of one of her friends, Holly's plan sprang into her mind again: "If you need the loo, always go in twos, understood?" She wished she'd bloody followed Holly's plan now. *Nothing to worry about, yet,* she told herself. Her friends were probably waiting outside, that's all.

As she walked towards the exit, she removed her iPhone from her satchel. No missed calls, no WhatsApp notifications, no messages. They obviously hadn't missed her. Looking around her, she decided to follow the crowd; after all, the caravan couldn't be *that* difficult to find.

Lauren loitered outside the bar for a few minutes, wondering why her friends had left her. Why hadn't they waited by the stage or thought to check the toilets? Why would they exit the venue without her? She glanced around, peering into the darkness, but she couldn't see them. There were a few people milling around – some leaving, some just getting there, plus a few smokers and some people who looked like they'd come out for some much-needed air, but none of these people were her friends. Where were they?

All of a sudden a strange, creeping sensation ran up Lauren's spine, and in an instant she remembered the shadowy man in the trees from earlier. It was the same feeling she'd had then – like she was sure she was being watched.

She glanced around her, looking at each and every face that passed her by, but every one of them was smiling, laughing, drunk.

And then she saw it: a shadow at the end of the building, the silhouette of a man, darting out of sight the instant she set eyes on him. She froze to the spot, her heart pounding. Was it the same man as before? Had he been watching her? Was someone actually following her?

Or was this just drunken paranoia, brought on by the fact that she couldn't find her friends? There were people everywhere, after all – it was probably just some drunk guy who was sneaking around the side of the building to go to the toilet or puke in the grass. Not everything had to be sinister, she reminded herself, laughing slightly at her overactive imagination.

Taking a deep breath, Lauren tried to clear her mind so she could think clearly. Then she started walking. She wished she'd noticed some of the landmarks when they'd first arrived; at least that way she would've been able to make her way home more easily. As she passed the man-made water fountain for the third time she became aware she was staggering and that she felt slightly dizzy. She shouldn't have drunk that last gin and tonic.

Veering off the main footpath, she took a leaf-carpeted path into the unknown, where old trees with their creaking branches swayed in the breeze. The smell of the woodland was delightful, the grass soft under her feet. A smattering of rain fell. Her foot caught on a crunching twig, making her jump. She looked up at the sky, asking for the heavens to help. The stars showered the night sky like transparent silver. As fog descended and her legs tired, the darkness cocooned her in a vacuum of silence.

She checked her phone: no signal. Then, in an instant, everything became pitch black – the light from her phone had vanished. *How did the bloody thing fall from her hand?* She searched on her hands and knees, the sodden ground feeling cold as it soaked through her jeans and stuck to her palms. Her hands moved in formation around her body, but there was no sign of it. Slowly creeping forwards, she repeated her movements. The tactic wasn't working. Standing up, she scuffed her feet out in front of her, a sense of hysteria making her heart beat faster. Her face dripped with sweat; she rubbed her hands across her brow as dread enveloped her. *No phone! No friends! No caravan! Lost!*

She stopped for a moment, taking a deep breath and deciding to retrace her steps, but it was no good – Lauren had no idea where she was, let alone her phone. So, she gave up trying to locate her mobile, deciding to look for it in the morning instead.

Morning! She wasn't even sure what time it was. Was she even going the right way? The darkness made her fearful. Where were her friends?

Suddenly she heard muffled voices, stopping Lauren in her tracks and freezing her to the spot as her mind wandered to the silhouette of the man she'd seen earlier. What if he'd followed her? What on earth would she do?

Then she realised it was only one voice – a voice asking for help.

"Hey, lady!" came a trembling cry. "Turn around, l-a-d-y!"

Lauren turned into the murkiness.

"Lady, help!" The voice was stronger now.

As Lauren squinted into the gloom the silhouette of a large man came into focus. A dim light from a nearby lamp post outlined another man on the ground. She shut her eyes and opened them again quickly, attempting to clear the blurry image from her mind. As she advanced towards the shape, all became clear.

A man was on his knees, stooped over a body on a muddy verge. There were stains on the man's shirt.

As Lauren approached she gasped, putting her hand to her mouth; both men were wearing bloodstained clothing. Should she stay put, run, or hide? No, the man needed help. She ran over.

"What happened?" Lauren fell to her knees as she looked at the man for a response.

"I saw him," the man said, "following you from the bar, and I thought he looked dangerous. I thought I'd check if you were okay, then I found him here on the floor. He's been stabbed." The man's words ran amok in her head.

"He was following me?" Lauren asked, eyes wide. "I thought I saw something, but I… I… how did he get stabbed?"

"I have no idea," the man replied, "I lost sight of him – and you – and when I found him again, he was already on the ground."

"Oh God," said Lauren, thinking how bad it could have been if the man had caught up to her – after all, he might have had a knife on him. "We need to call an ambulance," said Lauren urgently.

"I have. They're on their way." His eyes lingered on hers for a moment, a scared expression on his face.

The man on the ground looked like he was in his fifties. Lauren put her fingers onto his wrist to feel for a pulse – it was only faint, but at least he was still alive. She wished the ambulance would hurry up.

Just then flashing blue lights lit up the skies, the noise from the siren making her jump.

The next few minutes were a blur – a rush of panic as paramedics and police seized the area.

The paramedics helped the injured man onto a stretcher, clamping an oxygen mask to his mouth. After placing him gently into the ambulance they sped off, the siren echoing loudly down the muddy track.

A policeman was questioning the man Lauren had spoken to.

That man has a pleasant face, Lauren thought, the dim light outlining how attractive he was: big blue eyes, stubble, short cropped hair, and a small tattoo on his neck. Feeling compelled to find out his name, Lauren ambled over to the two of them.

"Will you need me to make a statement, officer?" she asked as she took another look at the handsome stranger.

"Yes please, madam. Both of you will need to come to the station," replied the officer.

"Of course. I'm Lauren, Lauren Adams." She held out her hand to shake the officer's hand. She wondered if it was the correct protocol, but he returned the gesture, shaking her hand vigorously.

Max wasted no time introducing himself. "I'm Max Davies, thank you for coming to help." Max held out his hand to Lauren, taking her focus off the policeman. When she held his hand in hers she could feel the roughness of his palms.

"I don't think I was much help, but thank you anyway," she said. Max's eyes locked on hers and for a brief moment she felt embarrassed. She released her hand from his grip.

"Officer," she said, turning back to the policeman, "I dropped my phone back there somewhere. Would it be okay if I have a quick search for it?"

"Yes, no problem – just don't touch anything else. We'll wait here. When you return, I'll drop you both to the station. Once you've made your statements you'll be free to go."

"I'll help you look," Max said as he caught up with her.

"There's no need."

"Don't want you getting lost too." Max smiled.

"I'm already lost," Lauren sighed.

"Sorry?" Max asked, frowning.

"Never mind. Can I call my number, from your phone?" Lauren knew this was an easy trick to see if hers lit up, and also a clever way to give Max her number.

"Sure, go ahead." Max handed Lauren his phone.

Lauren dialled her number and they stuck together like glue as they searched the area, waiting to hear a ringtone. No joy. Lauren soon realised it was a lost cause. She wasn't going to find it. Max agreed, so they made their way back to the waiting policeman.

As Lauren was being driven to the police station, with Max sitting by her side, she wondered – yet again – where her friends were.

Max, Earlier

Max walked out into the cool night air, his mind throbbing from one of his reoccurring headaches. He rubbed at his temples, attempting to soothe the pain. His plan was taking shape; he'd finally get to meet her. He'd already seen her at the bar. The black wig suited her. Her large hazel eyes had sparkled as she talked to the barman, an exuberant air of sophistication emitting from her tall, lithe body. What wasn't there to like about her?

In one hour the arranged meeting would take place. His visitor would be surprised. His idea of meeting here would kill two birds with one stone.

As the party atmosphere dissipated, Max felt relieved that his headache had almost gone. Now he could concentrate fully on the task in hand. The thinning crowd gave him the perfect view – all he had to do now was sit and wait.

Chapter Three

As Lauren walked out of the police station, the bright daylight obscuring her view, she abruptly turned around. She'd heard her name.

It was Max, his heavy breathing warm over her face as he spoke. "I just ran the whole of the corridor to get to you, Lauren Adams." Lauren was amazed Max had remembered her name. "Can I buy you a coffee?"

"I really need to get back to my friends; they'll be worried." *Bet they're not one bit,* thought Lauren, before having second thoughts. Something serious must've happened for her friends to abandon her like they had. One quick coffee wouldn't hurt, though – then she'd return to the caravan site. "Actually, that will be lovely, Max. Thank you."

"No, thank *you,* for last night. I mean, I don't know what I would've done without you." Max smiled at her.

"If I hadn't got lost and dropped my phone, I wouldn't have been there," Lauren replied, shrugging.

"I'm afraid the man was dead on arrival at the hospital," Max said abruptly, looking down at the ground.

For a second Lauren was at a loss for words. She felt numb. "I can't believe it, how sad. Will there be a murder investigation then?"

"I guess so," Max replied. "The police still want me to remain close by, for further questioning."

"You tried to save him; you're a hero," Lauren said quietly as she studied Max's face. She liked what she saw. She also wondered how Max had changed into clean clothes; the last time she'd seen him he'd been covered in bloodstains. The tattoo on his neck was intriguing. She wanted to ask about it, but she didn't dare.

"Well Lauren, shall we go for that coffee then?"

"You bet," she replied, cringing awkwardly at her words. Why was she talking in this unfamiliar language?

Together they walked to Caffè Nero, which was just across the road from the police station. It was busy with shoppers, needing their early morning caffeine fix.

"Grab that table by the window, Lauren," Max said, pushing her waist with his hands as he hurried her along.

Looking towards the window, Lauren realised it was her versus a man who was ogling the very same table. She almost ran like she was at an athletics meeting, dodging other tables and customers' feet to get there first, and when she did she sat down on the soft striped fabric of the chair feeling pleased with herself that she'd nabbed it. When she looked at her reflection in the window, however, her pleasure turned to horror; her make-up was smudged all over her face, and brown mud marks streaked down her cheeks. Wetting her fingers, she tried to rub them off but failed. She couldn't believe how awful she looked. She glanced up at Max, who had two cappuccinos in his hands.

"There you go. Looks like you need this – I certainly do."

"I need the bathroom," Lauren replied, standing up and hurriedly locating the toilets.

Once inside, she stood for a second, staring at the toilet mirror. Whatever did she look like? She turned the hot tap on to splash water over her face, ridding it of all the caked mud stains, then dabbed the excess water off with paper tissue. The dark circles under her eyes revealed her lack of sleep; four hours at the police station waiting to give her statement had clearly taken their toll. After tying her hair back and adding a touch of red lipstick, she looked – and felt – a little better.

As she stared at her reflection, she wondered if Max felt any attraction towards her. Looking at her face again in the mirror, she thought probably not. She definitely felt an attraction towards him, though. It had been instant and intense.

When she joined Max back at the table, she felt vulnerable; her usual sassy behaviour towards the opposite sex just wasn't happening.

"You look better. Revived, even," said Max.

"Not quite, but a shower and sleep will help."

Lauren sipped her tepid coffee as she listened to Max describing his life. He was a teacher working as a supply in several different schools. He loved the differentiated day and the challenges it bought, although now he mainly taught in primary schools. Lauren wondered how he covered up the tattoo he had on his neck; working in education, the dress code was always professional.

"Here's me going on and on," he said abruptly, "what about you?"

"Oh, my life's quite boring, really. I spend most of my time reading when I'm not working as a teaching assistant."

"Interesting." Max raised his right eyebrow.

"Not really. I haven't had the learning experiences you've obviously had."

"Yes you have – a teaching assistant's a rewarding job. I couldn't survive without a TA in my classroom. Teaching four-to-eleven-year-olds is a new experience every day. You can never fathom what questions children will ask. It's a learning curve in itself."

"That's true enough," Lauren admitted. "So, what made you go into teaching?"

Max thought for a moment before replying. "Every day it's an opportunity for me to inspire young people and give them the education they need to succeed in life. What about you? What made you want to become a teaching assistant?" Max was staring right into her eyes.

"The same really… for all SEND students to reach their full potential and to develop their independence," Lauren replied, smiling. She was glad she'd managed to match her answer with his.

She thought they could probably talk for hours, but with the coffees finished Lauren knew it was time to leave. She also had a phone she needed to buy; her withdrawal from social media had left her feeling incredibly isolated.

"Would you like to see me again, Lauren?"

Lauren liked Max's forthright question. "I'm only here for the weekend, but tomorrow is a possibility?"

"Sunday will be great for me. Shall we say twelve o'clock? We could meet by the pier on Minehead beach and go for lunch."

"It's a date then. See you Sunday – oh, and thank you for the coffee."

"You're welcome, Lauren."

They parted company, and once Lauren was out of sight Max pulled out the phone from his trouser pocket. Two faces looked at him from the screen saver: Lauren was smiling, the other girl poking her tongue out. Her friend, Max guessed. He snarled, his nostrils flaring as he remembered his time spent at Salford Primary School in Greater Manchester.

He put the phone back and patted his trouser pocket; he knew Lauren's phone would be safe there.

Chapter Four

Eighteen months ago

At the end of a long week, teacher Jessica Roberts leaned back into the leather chair in the corner of the staffroom, sighing loudly. Jessica had the makings of a wonderful teacher; although newly qualified, her professional approach was remarked on endlessly, and her rapport with the children had already gained her popularity. With her youthful looks she could easily be mistaken for a sixth-form student. Her long golden hair flowed down her back, almost to her hips; she'd only had it cut twice in all of her twenty-five years. A blunt fringe covered her forehead and freckles dotted her face. Her petite figure allowed her to wear anything imaginable.

"Are you okay?" Lauren asked her.

"I just had a weird conversation with a supply teacher," Jessica replied. "He called all the year sixes 'unintelligent' and 'idiots'. I don't think he's suitable for this school."

"You need to report him," said Lauren, who often listened to Jessica as she offloaded her problems.

Jessica frowned. "I don't think I should; as a new teacher, I don't really want to rock the boat."

"Well then, I'll do it for you. I'll tell Chris exactly what you told me. I'll go and see if he's free right now."

"Thank you, Lauren – only if you're sure you don't mind. I have a nasty suspicion about him. His name is Mr Reynolds."

Lauren knocked on the door to the principal's office. The sign displayed Chris Edward, Principal in gold writing. A sporty forty-seven-year-old, Chris had been principal of Salford Primary School for five years. His broad shoulders gave way to a sculpted body, and this – along with a curly mop of black hair and deep brown eyes – made him popular with the women. His customary pink and lilac shirts were the talk of the school staff.

"Come in." Chris looked up as Lauren entered the room. "Lauren, what can I do for you?"

As Lauren explained the inappropriate manner of the supply teacher, Chris leaned back into his recliner chair, shaking his head. "We cannot have unprofessional adults in this school. I'll get Candice to ring the agency and tell them we'll no longer need his services at Salford. Thank you, Lauren, for bringing this to my attention."

"No problem, Chris."

Lauren turned and walked towards the door, and just before she left, Chris called out, "You're an amazing teaching assistant, Lauren! You know that, don't you?"

"Of course." Lauren felt her cheeks redden as she closed the door behind her.

"All sorted, Jessica!" called Lauren as she popped her head around the door.

Jessica looked up and smiled. It was now four-thirty, and Lauren knew Jessica would remain in school until seven o'clock this evening, as she did most nights.

Tonight, though, Lauren was heading home on time. As she caught the bus on her usual commute from work, she thought about the guy she'd just complained about to Chris Edward. He wouldn't be working in education again, not if her complaint was heeded. To do this job, you needed to have a passion for the education system, and clearly, Mr Reynolds did not.

She smiled, glad she'd got rid of him; he wasn't going to return to Salford Primary School anytime soon.

Chapter Five

Lauren picked up a cheap pay-as-you-go mobile phone – not what she wanted, but it would do for now. When she returned to Manchester, she'd sort out a new one with a better contract. She couldn't believe she'd lost the other one – how careless of her!

Arriving by taxi to the caravan park, she was amazed by how different it looked in the daylight, and this time she had no trouble directing the driver to caravan seventy-six. All the other girls were sitting around the old wooden bench as she pulled up, Chloe the first one to give her a cheer as she saw who was arriving. When Lauren climbed out of the taxi, she ran over to give her a big bear hug.

"We've all missed you. What happened? Where've you been? We need the full story!" Chloe held Lauren's hand, pulling her over to the bench and patting the grey-stained slats, ushering Lauren to sit down.

"Not now, Chloe," Lauren said, exhausted. "Later. I need to sleep – wake me up at six." She walked past the other girls, noting the silence and their inquisitive looks. "I'm okay, really." She held her hands up in protest.

As soon as her head hit the pillow she relaxed, and it wasn't long before her eyes closed and she fell into a deep, dreamless sleep.

*****

As Lauren explained what had happened, she felt like she was the author of some kind of adventure story, her friends hanging off her every word. She exaggerated some parts, and she changed her tone every so often in order to engage them further.

As it turned out, Lauren's friends had had their own dilemma last night: Kate had been taken ill after mixing alcohol – far too much alcohol, by the sounds of it – with her medication. She'd had a bad reaction and had to be rushed to hospital. They'd tried ringing Lauren several times but couldn't get an answer. They even did a search of the bar area afterwards, and when they couldn't find her they'd guessed she'd gone back to the caravan. When they'd returned from the hospital to find Lauren wasn't there, they simply thought she'd met someone and had chosen to spend the night with him.

"What?" asked Lauren when she heard this part. "You know me, I never do that!" She thought for a moment, tilting her head as she added, "Well, just once, but only once in my entire life, and believe me, I never plan on doing it again. I can't believe you'd think I did that."

"Sorry," said Chloe, "but what else were we meant to think? You'd just completely vanished! Anyway, we were all so tired, what with going to the hospital and back…"

"I know," said Lauren, "you don't have to apologise. It sounds like we all had pretty rubbish nights."

"Still," said Holly, "we're sorry we didn't spend more time looking for you."

"It's fine, really," Lauren insisted, smiling at Kate and the rest of her friends. "I'm just glad Kate's okay. And besides, if I hadn't got lost, I wouldn't have met Max."

"So you've arranged to see this stranger again tomorrow?" piped up Chloe.

"Well, he's not exactly a stranger now," replied Lauren sarcastically.

"In my eyes he is," Kate agreed. "You know nothing about him."

"Well, that's why I'm meeting him, to get to know him better. Can you just leave it for now? I want to enjoy tonight with you guys – I've missed so much." Lauren was feeling so enthusiastic and energetic after her nap that she jumped onto Lucy's lap, cradling her arms around her neck. "Pretty please?"

Lucy laughed as she released Lauren's hands from around her neck. "Get off me, you idiot!" she screamed.

"Come on, let's get ready," said Holly. "I just hope tonight's better than last night. Now, we need to make a plan."

All the girls laughed together.

"You may laugh, but we need to think about our safety, especially now there's been a murder."

"There will be police patrolling the site – no need to worry." Chloe walked over to the kitchen, picked up the shot glasses, and opened the bottle of vodka. She then placed each one in a straight line on the worktop and filled them with the pure, clear liquid. "Come on girls, let's get this party started!"

With the radio blasting out loud music, the girls started getting ready, singing and dancing as they tried on their clothes and had the occasional shot. The outfits they'd brought with them certainly lived up to their gangster-inspired expectations – with trilbies, braces, and ties, it seemed like Bugsy Malone was in town.

When they were ready they made their way through the endless rows of modern caravans set among the mass of green turf. Some caravans looked like real homes – the gardens were immaculately kept, with all kinds of budding spring flowers about to erupt into a rainbow of colour.

All five girls walked with arms linked, making their way to the main stage area where the featured act of the night would play. Everyone seemed to be in a jovial mood, with strangers talking and laughing with each other.

"This is what I like most of all," said Holly, "everyone coming together."

Lauren nudged Chloe in the ribs, stifling a laugh. Chloe glared at her.

"I don't want Holly upset tonight," Chloe snapped at her. "Last night was bad enough."

Lauren frowned. She had the sense that something had happened between Chloe and Holly yesterday. "You're blaming me?" she asked.

"No, but Holly was grief-stricken and she didn't sleep all night – her plan for all of us to stick together failed."

"Sorry. I don't want anything to spoil tonight," Lauren said, giving Chloe a hug.

"You two okay?" asked Kate. "It's a lovely atmosphere here."

"We're okay," replied Chloe, smiling.

As the girls went from bar to bar, interest from the opposite sex followed them everywhere. The live band made an intoxicating atmosphere, the girls having no choice but to dance to the wonderful music. A trio of men with cheesy grins tried to hijack their group, and although they were slightly younger, the girls didn't care – they were game for a laugh.

It was two o'clock in the morning when everything closed down, and as people started to leave the three young men – Leo, Jack, and Steve – invited them back to their chalet for a party. The girls agreed, knowing that the chalets were all situated amongst the throng of nightlife. The men hadn't wanted a caravan that took half an hour to walk home to after a night out. Chalets cost double what the girls paid; Holly had decided it wasn't worth the cost just for somewhere to lay your head at night.

Leo was the best of the bunch, dark-featured and Italian-looking, his black stubble doing nothing to distract the girls from his amazing chocolate-brown eyes. His long eyelashes could be mistaken for false ones, and the dark line that contoured his inner eye line was black as black. He was of muscular build with olive skin, and his attention was most definitely focused on Lucy. She displayed her shyness – her face turning crimson every now and then – but she was clearly enjoying his company.

Jack was thickset with a neat light brown beard, and his dry humour produced bouts of laughter from everyone. Lauren didn't at all mind being snuggled up on the sofa with him under a blanket. Occasionally his hand would wander over her thigh, which would be her cue to get up and pour herself a drink.

This time she took it out onto the balcony. A table laden with alcohol and empty glass tumblers made her wonder how many drinks the men had put away before they'd gone out. They didn't appear to be intoxicated, though, just in a party mood.

"Did you have a party here before you went out tonight?" Lauren asked Jack as he appeared on the balcony and sat down next to her. Her eyes lingered on the table.

"No, that's yesterday's empties." Jack laughed.

"What made you want to come here for the weekend?" she asked.

"Same as you I expect… escapism."

"Maybe you're right," replied Lauren, "but I don't see it as that."

"Would you like to know me better?" Jack winked at Lauren. "What goes on in Minehead stays in Minehead."

Lauren smiled – she quite liked the attention she was receiving. "I'm not that sort of woman."

"Why not? I'm sure you've had offers before, a beautiful girl like you."

"Girl?" she laughed. "I'm almost a middle-aged woman, but thank you for the compliment. I'm getting a little chilly – shall we go back in?"

"Do we have to?"

"Yes," Lauren replied firmly, kissing Jack on the cheek.

As she walked back into the room, she clocked the time on the wall – thirteen minutes past four. She hadn't stayed out this late since she was a teenager. Everyone was still having a good time and she didn't want to be the one to spoil things. Lucy was engrossed in a conversation with Leo. It was good to see her enjoying herself. Lauren and Holly were playing a drinking game with Steve. Steve seemed to be the loser every time, much to his disgust. Kate was sitting quietly, sipping on water.

Holly and Kate were the first ones to call it a night, and after that, the party lost its enthusiasm. When Lauren, Lucy, and Chloe wanted to leave Leo and Jack insisted on walking them home, and as they stepped out of the boys' chalet, they realised dawn had broken.

"Whatever time is it?" asked Lucy as she walked unsteadily on her feet, hand in hand with Leo.

"Six thirty-two," said Lauren as she studied her watch. "Never before have I stayed out all night. This is a first for all of us, I think!" As Lauren yawned into her hand, Jack slipped his hand in her other one and squeezed it gently.

The site was quiet and the peace of the morning pleasant, void of all human activity. Birds were singing, and the sky had taken on a beautiful crimson colour. All the girls were dishevelled – hair out of place, make-up smudged – but they didn't care.

"This looks like we're doing the walk of shame," sniggered Lucy.

"Speak for yourself!" shouted Lauren.

The thirty-minute walk home turned into an hour's walk, and by the time they stepped through the door of the caravan it was seven-thirty, just in time for breakfast. Holly and Kate were sitting at the table, finishing their coffee and just about to grab a couple of hours' shut-eye – they'd been up all night too.

The raucous noise of the others arriving, however, changed their minds. Instead Holly offered their guests breakfast, and with two young men occupying their caravan it soon turned into another party, their humour filling the air with contagious laughter. Lauren was happy Holly was tied to the kitchen stove – she didn't fancy cooking a full English breakfast for seven. It would be no mean feat on a small oven, but Holly soon showed off her culinary expertise.

Once they'd all eaten, Leo and Jack thanked Holly for breakfast and the girls for a great night, saying they needed to go and get some sleep. There were no intimate goodbyes, just a friendly wave as they left. Holly, as usual, made a plan: get some sleep until lunchtime, and then pack. This time the girls were too tired to react to the standing joke and Holly looked bemused; for once, her plan was appreciated.

Lauren enjoyed the night but was looking forward to her impending date with Max. He was her last thought before she fell asleep.

Chapter Six

Lauren decided to play it cool. There was no need to go over the top – just keep it casual. Jeans and a camisole: plain, but comfortable. Her natural make-up highlighted her beauty. Besides, she couldn't fail to look better than she did the first time she'd met Max, when her hair was matted and her face covered in dirt. Max reminded her of a gladiator, although perhaps that was just the name – perhaps Max was short for Maximus. He was like her knight in shining armour, anyway. *I'm getting carried away,* she thought giddily.

Chloe dropped her off on the seafront, where people were already enjoying a lazy Sunday walk along the promenade in the warm September sunshine. A ridge of high pressure coming from the south-west had produced temperatures out of the norm for this time of year.

"Have fun – don't do anything I wouldn't do!" shouted Chloe.

"That doesn't leave me much to do then," Lauren said, winking at her friend as she shut the car door.

Flinging her small satchel over her shoulder, Lauren began making her way over to the clock tower, its bright emerald green paintwork shimmering in the sun. She noticed Max immediately; he was standing there with his hands in his pockets as he stared out to sea, his muscle-fit black T-shirt clinging nicely to his shapely torso. At the sight of him, a wave of excitement rushed through her body. She sneaked up to him and tapped him on his right shoulder.

He turned around, grinning from ear to ear. "Hi. Wow, you look gorgeous."

"Why thank you, Max. Where are you taking me then?" she asked coyly.

"Follow me." Max grabbed Lauren's arm, linking it through his.

Together they walked slowly through the middling crowd, and as they went Lauren couldn't help but feel like she'd known Max all her life; never before had she felt this way about a guy she'd only met twice.

They soon arrived at the Golden Plough, a public house and restaurant. Its immaculate grey and white painted stone walls looked enchanting. Outside, grey wooden benches sat at grey wooden tables, shadowed by large green canvas parasols.

They climbed the small narrow steps leading into the beer garden, where a handful of families were occupying the tables nearest to the small play area. As Max headed to a vacant table in the rear of the garden, he removed his arm from Lauren to hold her hand tightly.

"Will this table be okay?" asked Max.

"Perfect," replied Lauren quietly; all of a sudden she felt incredibly shy in front of him. She lifted her legs over the bench and sat down, relieved she was able to do it modestly and ladylike.

"What would you like to drink, Lauren?"

"A glass of red wine, please."

"Coming right up. I'll bring a menu."

She watched Max as he walked off towards the entrance to the bar. She could just make out the sign above the door: 'Spread love wherever you go, let no one ever come to you without leaving happier' – maybe this was an omen. She smiled. She also noticed several admiring glances from other women as they ogled Max strut across the vast lawn. Small daises were pushing through the orifices between the blades of grass. *What an exquisite place to be on a lazy Sunday lunchtime. Maybe getting lost on Friday night wasn't so bad after all,* she thought. Then she remembered the man who'd died that night and her face fell for a moment.

"Why are you looking so sad, Lauren?" Max asked as he placed the glass of wine and pint of beer down onto the table, spilling some of the beer as he sat.

"I was just thinking about the man who died on Friday."

"Me too. Horrible, isn't it? But let's not dwell – let's not spoil a lovely afternoon with great company."

"Me or you?"

"Me of course." Max stared into Lauren's eyes, though she didn't feel embarrassed this time; she quite liked it.

She laughed at him and then took a sip of her wine, letting the tannins invade her palate as she inhaled the sweet bouquet of the claret.

Max handed her the menu. "I think they only do a carvery on a Sunday."

"I love my Sunday roasts, so that will suit me just fine," said Lauren as she closed the menu, not even bothering to look.

"It looks to me like you don't eat enough of them. Do you work out?"

Lauren nearly spat out the wine. "Work out? You must be joking."

"I don't joke, Lauren." In an instant Max's voice had turned from a light jovial tone to one of aggression.

Lauren looked at Max, confused. After a moment she decided to forget his attacking tone for now, not wanting to ruin the moment. "I'll have the turkey roast then, please."

"In that case, so will I."

"Here, let me pay." Lauren fumbled about in her bag for her purse.

"No. I'll pay, Lauren. That's final," said Max with venom in his voice.

He walked off, leaving Lauren feeling slightly puzzled. She wondered what had just happened. She hadn't liked his mood just now.

When Max returned it was like nothing had happened at all, and his little outburst was soon forgotten. They laughed and talked, listening intently to each other as they discussed all kinds of topics. They enjoyed their carvery, and for dessert Max bought them chocolate fudge cake and ice cream, feeding Lauren small mouthfuls from his spoon. Lauren usually found it excruciating to watch when a romantic couple shared food with one spoon, but this time she loved it. Then, to burn off the excess calories, Max suggested a walk.

Walking hand in hand they ascended to the top of a tor, and for a moment they just sat and inhaled the beauty of the jaw-dropping scenery. Fields of green stretched on for miles and miles around, endless rolling hills that looked like something from a painting. Max talked for a moment about how he'd always loved the open countryside.

"You okay, Max?" asked Lauren. She'd noticed a kind of sadness in his eyes.

"Of course. Why shouldn't I be?"

There it was again – the sharpness in his voice. Lauren wondered if she was just being oversensitive. Max certainly had a serious side, though, and she was curious as to what had prompted it.

"Do you come from a large family, Max? Any brothers or sisters?"

"No. I'm an only child. My parents are dead."

"Oh – I'm sorry. I shouldn't be so nosy."

"That's okay, sweet. What about you?" Max took her hand and placed it in his, gently stroking the back of her palm while he waited for her to answer.

"I have one brother, Jacob; he lives in Canada, so I don't see him that often," Lauren replied with a heavy heart.

"Are you close?"

"Very. If I were ever in trouble, he'd help me out, no questions asked. I really miss him, but his career is so important to him. He works for a top recruitment firm, Fairfax Financial."

"I've heard of them. Good on him."

"You must meet him one day; I think the two of you would get on really well." As soon as she said the words, Lauren could have kicked herself. She was presuming too far ahead. Max might not even want to see her again.

"I'm sure we will, Lauren. Come on, I think it's time we got back." After pulling her up by her hands, Max lowered his face and his soft, smooth lips came into contact with hers. He pulled back and looked at her, waiting for a reply.

Lauren ran her fingers through his hair, then slowly kissed him to let him know their feelings were the same.

"I really want to see you again, Lauren. What do you think?" Max stared lovingly into Lauren's eyes, holding his stare.

"I think we can arrange that."

"You want to?"

"I'd love to," she replied, smiling. "I've had a great weekend meeting you, even though it was under awful circumstances… I still can't help thinking of the man that died."

"I know, me too. But he brought us together, and I will be eternally grateful to Thomas Victor for that." Max screwed his face up then, as if he'd been caught out.

"What did you say? You know his name?" Lauren asked, raising her eyebrows.

"I said I will always be eternally grateful to… the victim. I think his name was Thomas Victor – the police mentioned it in passing when they interviewed me."

"Oh," she replied, trying not to frown, before leaning over and kissing Max on the cheek. "Will you ring me?"

"Try and stop me."

A car horn sounding off alerted Lauren that Chloe was parked nearby, ready to pick her up, just as she said she'd be. She'd called Chloe after their lunch to see if she was available.

"I need to go."

"See you soon, Lauren."

"Bye."

Max stood and watched Lauren as she ran off. "You don't know what you're getting yourself into, Lauren Adams. You really don't," he muttered as his face contorted into a smirk.

Chapter Seven

After returning home from the weekend Lauren brooded for a while, snuggled up on the sofa with her favourite comfort blanket. She'd had this bit of rag for five years, and although it was regularly washed, it should have been banished to the rubbish bin – somehow, however, she couldn't bear to part from it. It was the first thing she'd reached for when her father had passed away. It had comforted her then, and it had continued to do so ever since.

Her father had been the centre of her universe, so when he was diagnosed with bowel cancer it felt like her world had ended. For quite a few days she hadn't known what to do; she'd walked in a trance, crying when she least expected it. Every Friday after work she had made the fifteen-mile journey to visit her parents, and staying in a village in the countryside was a kind of retreat for her. The idyllic small cottage had been a welcome distraction from work, allowing her to focus solely on her father. Slowly, day by day, her father had deteriorated. Always having been a strong, intelligent, capable man, he was now reduced to nothing more than a shell. His body, once fit and indestructible, was weaker than ever, though he still retained his remarkable young olive skin – the only thing that hadn't given way to the cruel disease. Her brother, Jacob, had remained in Canada. The cold winter months had turned her brother into a recluse, hibernating like a hedgehog until the spring months reappeared. His father was dying and he had chosen to simply block it out. It was his way of coping, Lauren guessed. The weekly update Lauren sent him was always returned with the same three words: *keep me posted.*

It wasn't that Lauren was resentful of being the only sibling who had to observe the worsening of their beloved father; it was more that she was worried about her brother. Brushing his feelings and emotions to one side was not doing Jacob any favours. He really should've just faced up to the inevitable.

Her mother had been the rock Lauren needed to lean on. Her father's wish was to die at home – he didn't want to be put into a hospice to fade away in front of strangers – so her parents made a pact. All his palliative care would be given at home. He'd never die alone.

Lauren recalled the time her mother had been struggling the most, a week after her father had been confined to his bed. Lauren had taken the decision then to stay at the cottage full-time, to support her mother and to say the goodbye to her father that she'd been prolonging. A release for his aged body was imminent. Lauren had needed to stay strong back then to keep her father's wish.

She remembered picking up a cotton bud from the bedside cabinet and dipping it into a jug of warm, clear liquid that was kept on the dresser. She'd watched as the bud absorbed the water, then she'd gently placed the damp bud along the contour of her father's cracked lips. The advice from the Macmillan nurse had been to do this every hour, and while she was happy to help, it was one of the most distressing things Lauren had ever done. She remembered this day like it was yesterday. The morphine had put her father into a comfortable place as his body gave up, and as he slowly slipped away, the peace that finally lay across his face had brought tears to her eyes.

Lauren stood up, pushing the blanket to the floor, and then made her way to the kitchen to get a glass of wine. She poured herself a large one before returning to the sofa and her blanket. Once she'd sat back down Max took over her thoughts, and she was glad for the interruption. She'd felt an instant connection with Max; it was the first time in a long time that she'd actually taken any real interest in a man.

Lauren had been looking for the man of her dreams all her life and now, she thought, she had found him. What should she do? Ringing him was out of the question – or was it?

"You're always too hasty, Lauren," she said out loud.

No, she'd wait.

Chapter Eight

Six Weeks Later

Lauren had just returned from another blissful weekend away with Max. Their relationship was flourishing; like new and excited lovebirds, they wanted to spend as much time with each other as they possibly could. Max was a gentleman, caring and loving, and their passionate trysts had developed into full-blown sexual encounters. Lauren had no reservations about her sexual desire for Max, even though she was not normally so intimate so early on in a relationship. With Max, though, it was different. It was special. Max made her feel confident, sexy, and happy. Max was for keeps.

Switching on the television and flicking through the channels until she found the news, Lauren flinched as a police mugshot filled the screen. The man looked so much like Max it was uncanny!

"Thomas Victor," announced the newsreader, *"aged fifty-nine, was stabbed to death at Butlin's, Minehead. Max Davies, forty-two, is wanted in connection with the killing."*

Lauren sat there with her mouth hanging open. No, it couldn't be...

"If you see this man," the newsreader continued, *"do not apprehend him. He is dangerous."*

Lauren stared at the photo of Max, the bright lights of the police camera making him look far paler than he usually was. It was definitely him, though, now that she looked closer – she'd know that even if she hadn't heard the newsreader say his name. Even in his mugshot he looked so handsome and innocent – surely this was all just a big mistake?!

Max? Dangerous? Lauren just couldn't believe it – how could this be? He'd helped save Thomas Victor, hadn't he? He certainly wasn't 'connected' with 'the killing', as the newsreader had put it.

I should know, she thought – *I was there.*

Over the last few weeks the police had asked her many questions regarding what happened on that night six weeks ago, and she'd freely answered them all, having nothing to hide whatsoever. She'd thought Max had nothing to hide, either; he too had been questioned, of course, but he'd never once mentioned that the police thought he was a suspect. Why would he keep this from her, especially as he *had* to be innocent?

Her Max wasn't a killer.

There was just no way.

They were wrong – they had to be.

*****

When Max walked into the police station in Manchester, it was of his own accord. He didn't want to wait to be arrested, and helping the police with their enquiries would show his cooperation. He opted for Manchester just so he could be close to Lauren.

He stood for a moment at the entrance to the police station, which was situated on a little side street just off the main road. How nice and neat it was, almost like an office setting. As he walked through the door, though, he grew anxious. *There's no turning back now.*

There were several chairs lined up along a back wall, a couple of leather armchairs sitting on their own in the corner. Several people were waiting to speak to police officers; it looked like a hospital waiting room, though there were posters about criminal activities pinned to a large noticeboard instead of notices about medical issues. Looking forward, Max saw some sliding frosted doors. There was an officer sitting behind the information desk, busy writing something down. Max slowly approached the officer and coughed lightly, trying to gain his attention.

"Can I help you?" The officer looked Max up and down.

"I'm Max Davies. I've come here to help with the investigation regarding the death of Thomas Victor."

"Take a seat, Sir. Somebody will be out to see you soon."

"Thank you."

Max sat down on the cold imitation leather chair and waited.

Suddenly the sliding doors squeaked open and a short, stocky man dressed in full uniform and carrying a clipboard walked towards Max. "Mr Max Davies," he announced.

"Yes." Max could feel several pairs of eyes boring into him, people nudging each other as their eyes flickered between him and the small TV screen. When he looked over, he saw his name being flashed all over the news channel.

"Would you like to follow me, Sir?" smiled the officer.

Max stood up, grateful for the stretch to his calf muscles, and then followed the officer through the sliding doors. It felt like he was stepping through some kind of time zone; the chaotic buzz of excitement here was so different to the calm environment on the other side of the doors.

"Mr Davies, do you want a solicitor to be present?" asked the officer. "If so, waiting for one will take longer. If you want this matter dealt with quickly, we can go ahead without one."

"There's no reason for a solicitor to be present," Max replied. "I have nothing to hide; that's why I came here today." He kept his voice level and steady, knowing he had to play it cool.

The officer took Max over to a desk, where he had to undergo the booking process, including getting fingerprinted and photographed. He felt like a criminal already. After this, he was left alone again to wait.

As time passed, his nerves began to kick in and his palms began to sweat. Max imagined that this was probably police protocol, to make you feel uneasy and intimidated. A tactic, to try to make you nervous. To make you say something you shouldn't. To make you slip up.

"Mr Davies, please follow me," the officer said, walking over to a door and opening it. "Take a seat in here, Sir; Detective Biggs will be with you shortly."

It was a small room, containing only three chairs and a desk. Nothing hung on the grey stone walls. It gave a sense of exposure and isolation. In a matter of minutes, in walked the detective.

Detective Stephen Biggs took long strides to the desk, Max's first impression being that he was definitely a man of power. He was of dual-heritage, and considering that his six-foot two-inch frame towered over most people, he had immediate power in his role of negotiator/officer. His body language displayed confidence and self-assurance, his face harsh on the eye. Cheekbones jutted outwards, and a wide forehead revealed deep lines embedded in his dark skin. A few age spots blotted his complexion. A gold front tooth sat neatly in between his white veneers, a small Afro claiming his Caribbean roots.

He took a seat opposite Max. "Mr Davies, I'm Detective Biggs." He held his hand out to Max, and Max returned the friendly gesture, shaking his hand firmly. "I hear you want to tell us about what happened on the night of September fourteenth?"

"That's right." Max sat upright in his chair as he stared menacingly at Detective Stephen Biggs, trying to throw him off guard. The detective simply stared back at him, saying nothing. "I heard you wanted to talk to me about it, so here I am."

"Great," said Detective Biggs, leaning back in his chair. "Does this mean you've got something to add to your original statement?"

"Well," said Max, fidgeting with his hands, "I wouldn't say that exactly. Well, maybe. I mean..." He laughed nervously, his voice shaking as he shrugged his shoulders. "Sorry," he added, "I just hate police stations."

As Detective Biggs stared at him, Max wondered if his little nervous routine was working. He'd been watching a lot of American TV dramas recently, especially ones involving police procedure, and he'd made a list of all the different tactics he could use during a police interview. One of them was to act guilty, confusing Biggs and hopefully luring him into a false sense of security. He knew the detective wanted a confession, and while Max wasn't going to give him that – not if he could help it, anyway – he wanted the detective to *think* he was on the verge of confessing.

Detective Biggs could sense the nervousness in Max's body; it was crying, *Get me out of here!* as he fidgeted in the uncomfortable chair. Biggs could tell that Max was aware of

51

the one-way mirror, and – from experience – he knew it would heighten his anxiety. He had already worked out Max's plan, so now he was going to try his own.

"Just relax," he told Max, his voice friendly and soothing. "You came to us, remember? So just say what you've got to say, and you can be on your way." The detective smiled at him, as though this were nothing more serious than a job interview or two friends meeting over coffee.

Slowly and carefully, Biggs began to create a rapport with Max, making him believe he was on his side. Biggs was well trained, and when Max was remembering and recalling past events, he noticed that his eyes were moving to the right. Most defendants did this when they were lying. He made a note of it in his notepad.

"So," said Biggs after Max had recounted the story of that night again, "let's go back and start from the top again."

"What?" asked Max. "Why?"

Biggs shrugged. "I just need to hear the story again – if you don't mind."

"Okay," replied Max, feeling a little unsure of himself now. What game was Detective Biggs playing?

Biggs pretended to write down notes as Max spoke, intentionally making concerned facial expressions every now and then, as though something didn't make sense to him. "Are you sure?" he asked, interrupting Max's explanation for the fourth or fifth time.

"Sure? Sure of what?" Max asked, frowning.

"It's just, before, you said that you saw Lauren Adams first, before you heard her scrambling around. This time, you said you heard someone and then looked over to see her. Which way round was it?"

Max frowned again. "Does it matter? I can't remember."

"I see," said Biggs, making a note in his book. "So if you can't remember that, does it mean you can't remember other things as well?" Biggs looked up from his notepad. "Am I getting the full story here, Max?"

"Yes," said Max, "I mean no. I just mean… I saw and heard Lauren at the same time, okay? Though I don't see what difference it makes."

Biggs shrugged. "It could make no difference, or it could make all the difference in the world. I just have to make sure your statement's the same as the first one you gave. Otherwise… well, we could have a problem, and we don't want that, do we?"

"Right," said Max, "well, I've gone through it twice now, so can I go?"

Biggs looked back at his notepad again, shaking his head. "I'm afraid you've given me three different versions of that night now – we can't stop until you remember which one is correct."

Max gritted his teeth. "I really don't see how it can matter that much whether I saw or heard Lauren first, okay?"

Biggs looked back through his notes. "It's not just that… there are several inconsistencies here. Start again."

"What?" Max couldn't believe what he was hearing.

"Start again," Biggs repeated, still staring down at his notepad. "Right from the top. Please."

Max held his head in his hands, his shoulders hunched forward. He was beginning to lose control. After taking a deep breath, he sat up straight, trying to regain his composure.

Finally looking up from his notepad, Biggs stared into Max's eyes long and hard, seeing that his eyes were watering. He was making a breakthrough at last.

Biggs continued to combine real questioning with irrelevant questioning, leading Max to believe that he had something on his mind, while also making him tell the same story over and over again. As he did so, he kept checking Max's body language. He was sitting back in the uncomfortable chair with his hands crossed, and every time Biggs asked him a question Max got into a defensive position, tilting his head to the right – this usually meant the suspect was trying to think of an answer. Max used the word 'honestly' several times, revealing that he was lying. Describing minor details of how he found Thomas Victor lying on the floor, stabbed, also revealed he was a liar. No one adds minor details to a statement unless they're asked, just the major details. Biggs knew he was onto a winner.

"Repeat the story again, Max – if you would." Biggs added in this last part to give Max a little bit of respect. He still needed him on side if he was going to get the truth out of him.

Then, Biggs let Max talk and talk. It was one of his most successful strategies: get the defendant to talk, without any interruptions, and eventually they would reveal what they actually knew.

After several hours another detective entered the room, leaning down and whispering into Biggs' ear. Biggs gave Max a short look, then excused himself. "I'll be back in five minutes," he told Max. "While I'm gone, why don't you think about the moment you first saw Lauren again? See if anything comes back to you."

A whole hour passed before Biggs returned. He sat down opposite Max and rearranged a few things on the table. He then wrote something down in his black notebook.

"That was a long five minutes," Max said.

Biggs didn't reply.

The look on Max's face was one of pure worry, Biggs could tell. This little interruption to the questioning had gone to plan – it was another strategy that always worked.

Biggs continued to interrogate Max, slowly becoming Max's friend while at the same time making him go over and over his statement until he was so muddled he could barely think straight. While he did this, the detective used the minimisation technique, downplaying the seriousness of the situation and saying it wasn't Max's fault.

"You and I both know," he told Max, "that you were simply in the wrong place at the wrong time, that was all."

This technique usually worked, and it did this time too.

After sixteen hours of intense interrogation, Max had confessed.

Chapter Nine

For one hundred and twelve days, Max had been on remand in HM Prison Manchester.

He had the ranking of a category A prisoner – which meant no bail conditions – and he was sharing a cell with a convicted prisoner. He tried not to speak to his cellmate if he could help it. He tried not to speak to anyone in that cold, gloomy place.

Although he couldn't be released on bail, his rights allowed him letters, telephone calls, and visits from Lauren. She contacted him as often as she could, always asking how he was and always saying how she couldn't wait for him to come home. Lauren was the only one he would speak to.

She was allowed to see Max for ninety minutes a week, and she made sure she went every week – she just couldn't bear to be apart from him. As well as the weekly visit, a daily phone call was her lifeline, and she often spent the day counting down the hours and minutes until she could hear Max's voice.

Despite everything that had happened, Lauren was just as smitten as ever; she knew that when they'd locked eyes for the very first time that fateful evening – and when everything around her had slowed down, like she was in a movie – he was the one. She knew again when Max had kissed her for the first time and her breath had caught, making her head swoon. Yes, this was definitely something more than a passing fling, and not even prison could put a stop to her feelings for him.

Besides, she wouldn't have to wait much longer. His innocence would soon be uncovered, and then he'd come back to her, back to her loving arms; she had no doubt in her mind that Max wasn't guilty. He wasn't a murderer! He would never harm a fly, let alone kill anyone. In Lauren's eyes, he was simply perfect.

Yes, she told herself, soon he would be freed, and then they would be together forever.

A long seven months passed before the trial started.

Chapter Ten

The court clerk asked Max if he was ready, and in response Max – who was flanked by prison officers – smiled, nodding his head to signify he was all set. The clerk selected the jury panel numbers, calling them out one by one as the jurors took themselves to the jury box. The stenographer was on hand to record everything that was said. It was time.

The courtroom gleamed, the light from the large strip lights bouncing off the polished sheen of the mahogany tables and chairs. The red and black tapestry carpet was pristine. A couple of opaque marble columns added a sense of roman architecture to the large space, the spotlights and the diamond-shaped chandelier hanging above the Queen's Bench setting a peaceful tone.

When Max woke that morning he knew it was going to be a good day. His head was in a good place and he felt confident the verdict would go his way. The black and grey conservative suit he'd chosen would show the judge and jury respect. He'd even covered his tattoo with a plaster.

After being searched by an officer Max was told to go and sit in the dock, which was situated at the side of the courtroom. Judge Walters entered the court and Max was told to stand. The court clerk made his way over to the dock.

"Can you please tell the court your name and address?"

"Max Davies, Thirty-two Ridgeway Road, Islington, Greater London."

"Are you maintaining your not guilty plea?"

"Yes."

"You may sit down."

Twelve jurors were all individually sworn in, all of them required to take the oath or to affirm. Max eyed each one of them, happy to see that the majority of them looked like they would try him fairly on the evidence they'd hear. None of them were scowling at him anyway.

The court clerk then identified Max to the jury before reading out his charge. As Max heard the words he stared straight ahead, keeping his head held high.

Judge Walters was a heavyset man with grey hair and a matching beard, his tanned, leathered face showing a life well lived. His glasses were perched on the edge of his nose as he addressed the jury. "You, the jury, fulfil a very important function today. You have the responsibility of deciding whether, based on the facts of this case, the defendant is guilty or not guilty of the offence for which he has been charged. You must reach the verdict by considering only the evidence introduced in court. You must not discuss this case with anyone else, unless with your fellow jurors in the jury room, and you must not conduct your own independent research about this case. Do you understand?"

The jury spokesman stood up and replied, "Yes your honour, we understand."

"Defence and prosecution, are you ready to make your opening statements?"

David Grainger and Penelope Miller both stood up.

"Yes, your honour," answered David Grainger.

"Yes, your honour," answered Penelope Miller.

"In that case, Mr Grainger, please begin."

David Grainger nodded, cleared his throat, and then turned to face the jury. "Good afternoon, ladies and gentleman. My name is David Grainger, and I am representing the defendant, Max Davies. We are here today to decide if the defendant committed murder. On the night of September fourteenth, Mr Davies was at Butlin's holiday park, Minehead, alone. He attempted to save the life of Thomas Victor. In this trial I will provide police reports, including the pressured confession of my defendant, which will illustrate his innocence. Ladies and gentleman of the jury, Mr Davies is a hardworking, honest, law-abiding citizen. He is a schoolteacher, dedicated to encouraging his students to be the best they can be. He is not a murderer. At the conclusion of this trial, it is my hope that in the interests of justice you will find that the defendant is not responsible for the death of Thomas Victor. Thank you." David Grainger nodded to the judge and jury before sitting down.

Grainger had expert analytical and interpersonal skills and was incredibly effective in the courtroom, making convincing arguments to both judges and juries alike. In his mind, today would be no exception.

Next, Penelope Miller took to the floor. "Good afternoon, ladies and gentleman. My name is Penelope Miller, the prosecution lawyer for this trial. On the night of September fourteenth, the defendant Max Davies committed the crime of murder. The defendant's own confession – and the weapon found at the scene of the crime – will prove to you that the defendant is guilty of the murder of Thomas Victor. Thank you."

Penelope Miller kept her opening statement short; she would do her real damage during the trial.

*****

Lauren waited and waited. She wished they'd hurry up. Ninety minutes she'd been sitting on the rigid high stool with a dry mouth and sweaty palms. It hadn't been a good idea to wipe her hands on her pale mint bodycon dress; now there were two damp patches right down the centre. She hoped they would dry before she entered the courtroom.

"Lauren Adams!" A short man, who had wide-rimmed glasses and a fringe swept back over his balding head, called her name. He was dressed in a neat formal suit.

As Lauren stood up she glanced down at her dress, the two damp patches remaining there for judge and jury to see. She was already on the back foot – not ideal for her first court appearance.

As the court clerks showed her to the witness box she felt everyone's eyes upon her, but although she was nervous, she didn't let it show; her body language displayed confidence and assuredness as her heels made a short, sharp sound along the tiled floor. Inside, she was shaking.

When she was asked to take the oath Lauren replied, "I affirm," and as she looked across to the dock at the back of the court her eyes shot towards Max's face. He looked pale and drawn, and it hurt her heart to see him like this.

Standing up, Penelope Miller walked towards the judge before swivelling around on her four-inch patent black heels. Her thin face was speckled with light brown spots, her close-set piercing brown eyes staring into Lauren's.

"Lauren Adams, you first met the defendant at Butlin's holiday park, Minehead, on September fourteenth. Is that correct?"

"Yes, that's right."

"What happened on that night, Ms Adams? Please tell the court."

"Well, that night I got lost and dropped my phone. As I was trying to find it, I heard voices."

"Voices, Ms Adams?" Penelope Miller asked, raising her eyebrows.

"I mean, *a voice* – it turned out to be his voice." Lauren turned her head slightly, looking over at Max.

"You mean the defendant, Mr Max Davies, Ms Adams?" Penelope Miller asked impatiently.

"Yes."

"Tell us what happened next, Ms Adams." Penelope Miller sliced her eyes at Lauren, making her feel uneasy.

"Max – I mean, Mr Davies – called out for help. I saw a man crouched over another man on the ground, and I went over to see if I could help."

"A man crouched over another. Was this man the defendant, Mr Max Davies?"

"Yes, it was." Lauren replied, enunciating each of the three words loudly and clearly. "He said he thought the man had been following me, and that he wanted to check I was alright."

Miller stared at her for a moment. "He believed someone was following you, so he also chose to follow you?"

"To help me," Lauren pointed out.

"And is it true," Penelope Miller continued, "that you were the only person to witness this?"

Lauren nodded.

"Is that a yes, Ms Adams? Please state for the court."

"Yes," replied Lauren in a rather sarcastic tone.

"Was the defendant holding a weapon? A knife?"

"No, he was not."

"But it was dark, you may not have noticed."

"Objection, your honour!" David Grainger shouted as he rose from his seat.

"On what grounds?" asked Judge Walters.

"There is no evidence that Mr Davies was holding a weapon."

"Sustained." Judge Walters removed his glasses and waved them in the air, gesturing for them to move on.

"Ms Adams, when you saw Mr Davies, was he in an agitated state?" Penelope Miller asked as she walked towards Lauren in the witness box, waiting for her reply.

"I wouldn't say agitated, but he was obviously distressed about the situation he'd found himself in."

"Aren't agitated and distressed the same thing? In my mind they are." Penelope Miller turned around again, walking away from the witness box.

"Not in mine," Lauren replied. "Agitated means feeling nervous, while distressed means suffering from extreme pain or sorrow." *Touché,* she said quietly in her head.

"Are you covering for your lover, Ms Adams?"

"Objection, your honour!" David Grainger looked livid.

"Sustained. Ms Miller, please refrain from putting suggestions into the minds of the jury."

"Apologies, your honour." Penelope turned back to face Lauren. "Can you tell the court what you were doing at the Butlin's holiday park?"

Lauren stared at her, unsure what to say – was this some kind of trap? "Well," she said eventually, "I was on holiday."

A quiet sniggering sound came from someone near the back of the court, but Penelope Miller ignored it as she continued her questioning.

"Who were you there with?"

"I was there with four of my friends," Lauren replied.

"And where were these friends when you came across the defendant?"

"They… they weren't there. As I said, I got lost on the way back to the caravan."

"Which is when you stumbled upon Max Davies?"

"Yes," Lauren replied, glancing at Max and his lawyer. Where was she going with this?

"Can anyone confirm this?"

"Confirm what?" Lauren asked, shifting slightly on her seat. She could feel a trail of sweat making its way down her back.

"That you found Max Davies next to the body, and that this was the first time you two had ever met?"

Lauren's face coloured as she realised what Miller was getting at. "If you think I had something to do with that poor man's death," she said angrily, "then you must be insane."

"Insane?" questioned Penelope Miller. "How so? A man is dead, and you and the defendant were the only people found at the crime scene. That's a fact, Ms Adams – not insane at all."

Lauren started to speak, then stopped. She was flustered, and scared, and had absolutely no idea what she should or shouldn't say. She'd been spending so much time worrying about Max and trying to prove his innocence – she hadn't once thought that she might have to try and prove her own!

The silence in the courtroom stretched out as Miller stared at Lauren, clearly waiting to see if she would continue talking and somehow incriminate herself.

"Do you have a question for the witness?" the judge asked Miller eventually, sounding a little annoyed at the delay.

"Yes," Miller said, taking a step closer to the witness stand. "Did you know Max Davies prior to meeting him at the Butlin's holiday park?"

"No," Lauren said, her voice shaking slightly.

"So you were not secretly there *with* Max Davies?"

"What? No!" Lauren replied, frowning in confusion.

"And if you weren't there with Max Davies, are you saying you had no hand whatsoever in the death of Thomas Victor?"

"Of course not!" Lauren said, her forehead starting to perspire now too. "You didn't even find my fingerprints on the knife!"

"No," agreed Miller, "but we did find Max's prints on the knife. Are you saying he did kill Thomas Victor?"

"No, I… that's not what I'm saying at all."

"So you know nothing about this knife?"

"No! I don't know anything about the goddamn knife!" Lauren shouted, standing up from her seat.

There was silence in the courtroom again as everyone stared at Lauren.

"Objection, your honour," Grainger said softly into the silence. "Ms Miller is badgering my witness."

Penelope Miller smiled, saying, "I have no more questions at this time," before the judge even had a chance to respond. She knew she'd achieved her tactical plan; in her eyes, she had completely discredited the witness. The jury would think twice about trusting someone as nervous and easy to anger as Lauren Adams. She walked happily back to the bench.

Lauren took several deep breaths. She'd expected it to be difficult in the witness box but she hadn't expected Penelope Miller to be quite so intimidating. She also hadn't expected to spectacularly lose it while she was on the stand.

Fortunately, David Grainger's questioning of her was short and sweet, over in just a few minutes. But still she couldn't stop thinking about the way she'd reacted to Miller's questions; when Lauren left the witness box, she cringed inwardly, unable to even look Max in the eye as she walked back to her seat.

Max wasn't required to present evidence at the trial, but he'd decided to do so anyway. His lawyer agreed – if he gave his account of what happened that night, the court could hear it in his own words, and would be sure to name him not guilty.

David Grainger walked towards the bench. "I would like to call my client, Max Davies, to the stand."

Max came waltzing out from the dock to the witness box, standing up straight with his shoulders pushed back, oozing confidence.

"Mr Davies, where were you on the night of September fourteenth?" David Grainger asked, wasting no time.

"I was at Butlin's holiday park, Minehead," Max replied, his voice assertive and strong.

"Did you go to the holiday park with anyone?"

"No, I was alone."

"You went to an adult weekend alone? Can you tell the court why?"

"It was a spur-of-the-moment thing. I had nothing else planned. It's a good weekend to meet different people."

"I see. And can you tell the court what happened that night?"

"On the night of September fourteenth I left Reds bar to grab some fresh air – it was so stuffy in there, I felt a migraine coming on. I noticed a man following a woman, and something didn't seem right, so I followed. I lost them for a bit but then I suddenly heard a muffled voice that seemed to be groaning. I went to investigate and I found a man spread out on the floor."

"You mean Thomas Victor?" asked David Grainger.

"Yes, Thomas Victor. It was quite dark, only a dim light from a nearby lamp post helped me to see anything. I noticed a stain on his shirt and realised it was blood. It looked like he'd been stabbed."

"Stabbed? Where, Mr Davies?"

"In the stomach. I pressed on the wound to compress the bleeding but it wouldn't stop."

"Did you ring for an ambulance?"

"Yes. As soon as I couldn't stop the bleeding, I rang for an ambulance," Max explained.

"Please carry on, Mr Davies," said Grainger.

"I called the ambulance, and then a young woman appeared – the one I thought the man had been following – so I called out for help."

"The young woman being Ms Lauren Adams?" David Grainger pointed his finger straight at Lauren, reminding the jury of who she was.

66

"That's correct."

"Thank you, Mr Davies. I have no further questions, your honour."

Penelope Miller stood and walked straight to the witness box, staring at Max head-on. "Mr Davies, can you explain to the court why you didn't immediately ring for an ambulance upon finding Thomas Victor bleeding on the ground? Why did you wait?"

"As I said before," said Max, sounding a little irritated, "I tried to suppress the bleeding. I was trying to save his life."

"But wouldn't ringing for an ambulance be trying to save his life too? Wouldn't that have been the most sensible approach? Have you had any first aid training before?" She fired off the questions rapidly, hoping to catch him out.

"No, I haven't – but I thought I was doing the right thing."

"You thought you were doing the right thing, but it wasn't the right thing, was it, Mr Davies? If you'd called for an ambulance right away, Thomas Victor could have lived. If you'd done the most logical thing – the thing anyone else would have done – he'd still be alive right now."

"Objection, your honour," said Grainger, "that is a hypothetical statement."

"Sustained," Judge Walters replied, appearing annoyed. "Please stick to the facts, Ms Miller."

Miller nodded. "Why did you pick up the knife and throw it away? Didn't you think it would be used as evidence, Max?" Penelope Miller liked to sway between using the first name of a defendant and then switching to their surname. It threw them off balance, and she could tell Max was rattled.

"It was lying there next to the body – with blood all over it. It was just my instinct to get rid of it. I didn't want it getting in the way as I tried to suppress the blood."

"Really? But wasn't it dark, Mr Davies? How did you see there was 'blood all over it'?"

"Objection, your honour! Ms Miller is implying my client is lying." David Grainger was livid, his face red, his brow furrowed.

"Overruled." Judge Walters had no hesitation in his decision.

"I can remember seeing the blood on the knife – it's given me nightmares to this very day." Max moved his hand to his eye, wiping away a tear.

Ignoring the show he was putting on, Penelope Miller continued. "Mr Davies, can you tell the jury why you didn't shout for help? This was a busy weekend, surely there would have been people around?"

"I did – that was when Ms Adams heard my appeal for help," Max pointed out.

"But wasn't that a little too late?" Miller asked as she began to stride up and down the courtroom.

"My main objective was to try and save Mr Victor," Max explained. "Screaming for help would've distracted me from trying to do this, don't you think?" He was pleased at how he was answering the bitch. He needed to stay calm, though; he didn't want to give the jury any reason to doubt him.

"Is it true, Mr Davies, that you and Ms Adams are in a relationship?"

"We have become close since we met," Max replied.

"Let me put it more simply – are you and Ms Adams in a sexual relationship?"

Lauren felt her cheeks burning as people turned to stare at her.

"Objection, your honour – this question is irrelevant to the facts." Again, David Grainger was on his feet.

"Sustained. Ms Miller, please adhere to the facts. This is your first warning."

Miller nodded before continuing. "The biggest piece of evidence we have in this case is your confession to Detective Stephen Biggs."

Max shifted on his seat, clearly uncomfortable now.

"Can you tell me why you're pleading not guilty when you've already confessed to the murder of Thomas Victor?"

Max lowered his head, willing himself to start crying – if he strained his eyes enough, he knew he could squeeze a few tears out.

"Mr Davies, please answer the question," the judge stated after a moment.

When Max looked back up, his eyes were filled with tears. "I didn't kill him," he said quietly. "I only confessed because I was confused."

"Confused?" Miller repeated, raising her eyebrows. "Why were you confused?"

Max stared directly at the lawyer as he said, "Have you ever been interrogated for sixteen straight hours? They made me go over my statement so many times that by the end of it I barely even knew where I was. I was tired and hungry and thirsty, and I just wanted it to end – I would have said anything they wanted to hear to get out of that small, cold room." He stared at the jury then, looking at each of their faces in turn. "They made me say those things."

"And yet," said Penelope Miller, "you still said them. You still confessed to murder. No further questions, your honour." She smiled at Max as she walked back to her seat.

"You may step down from the witness box," said Judge Walters.

Max walked past the jury, remaining sombre. His head was telling him he'd nailed this – after all, he still had tears on his cheeks, showing how sorry and distraught he was by this whole thing. The jury couldn't help but feel sorry for him, surely?

After a few moments, the court clerk held up a document file. "I have here item number one, a document submitted by Detective Stephen Biggs, detailing the interview he conducted with the defendant. I shall now read it out for the court to hear."

As the confession was read out it drew several gasps from the jury, some of them exchanging shocked glances as they heard Max's words – as they heard him confess to the murder of Thomas Victor.

A worried Lauren looked over at Max, who'd started to sweat. Clearly, he was scared for the verdict.

She was too.

*****

Finally, it was time for the conclusion of the trial, and Penelope Miller was preparing herself for her closing statement. She had just five minutes to expose Max Davies, once and for all, as the guilty man he was.

"Members of the jury, your honour, today we've heard the account of what happened on September fourteenth. We've heard it from Mr Davies himself, and then from his previous recorded confession. These accounts, as you've heard, do not match."

Penelope Miller stared at the jury, her gaze searching along the front pew from left to right. After a moment she focused on a middle-aged man with receding grey hair. His round freckled face screwed up as he smiled back at her.

"Max Davies failed to ring for an ambulance immediately after coming across Thomas Victor, an act that could have saved his life. Surely, in such circumstances, this would be the first thing you would do." The middle-aged man nodded in agreement.

Penelope Miller walked down to the opposite end of the jury, this time focusing on a young brunette. "Ms Lauren Adams claims she found Max Davies hunched over Thomas Victor, trying to suppress his wound. It was dark apart from the dim light coming from a nearby lamp post. Could Ms Adams really have seen Max Davies trying to help? The knife that killed Thomas Victor was found to have the defendant's fingerprints over the handle. He picked the knife up and discarded it, and he neglected to notify the police about the weapon when he was helping with their enquiries. Is this something you would forget to disclose? I think not." The brunette nodded in agreement.

"We also know that Max Davies actually confessed to this murder during an official police interview. Need I say more?" She shrugged her shoulders. "I put forward," Miller continued, "that Max Davies stabbed Thomas Victor on the night of

September fourteenth. He threw away the knife because he knew it would incriminate him in the murder. When he became aware of Ms Lauren Adams in the vicinity, he asked for help in a bid to cover his tracks." She walked right over to the jury, staring at them each in turn. "Max Davies is a cold, ruthless killer who deserves to go to jail for this brutal crime. Your honour, the jury, I hereby end my closing statement."

Penelope Miller walked back to her desk, avoiding eye contact with anyone as she sat down.

Next, David Grainger walked to the centre of the court, his tall frame exuding professionalism. "Your honour, the jury, I plead that the defendant Max Davies is innocent. On the night of September fourteenth, by accident, Mr Davies came across a dying Thomas Victor and did the decent deed of trying to save his life. He didn't have to do this; he could have easily walked away. But Max Davies, who is a credible, hard-working professional and a well-respected citizen, chose not to. Instead he chose to stop and help a human being in need. In hindsight, Max knows he was wrong to discard the alleged murder weapon, but when you're put on the spot and are in a tense situation, your mind does not always see reasoning. He acted instinctively, wanting to get the murder weapon away from the bleeding man in front of him. Frantically trying to stem the blood flow from a victim's wound is a heroic act, and it displays Max's caring attitude towards others. Max's thumb and forefinger prints that were found on the knife only demonstrate how the defendant tossed the knife away aimlessly, suggesting this was an act of pure innocence. The knife landed in a wooded area. Surely, if Max Davies was guilty of foul play, he would've abandoned the knife more securely than he had, perhaps by burying it in the ground. Instead, he left it out in the open, for anyone to find. These are not the actions of a guilty man. His confession was subject to intense pressure from an interrogation, initiated by Detective

Biggs. I request you set a verdict of not guilty. Your honour, the jury, I hereby end my closing statement."

As David Grainger walked to his seat he gave a wry smile to Penelope Miller, who – for once –looked nervous.

To end the session, Judge Eric Walters announced to the jury that they must make their decision based only on the facts presented, and that they weren't to let their feelings cloud their judgement. Max watched the jurors' faces with interest, his gaze following them as they stood and left the room.

He could do nothing more now.

*****

Two hours later everyone was back in the courtroom, awaiting the verdict; it had taken the jury just one hour and fifty-minutes to make their decision.

When Max heard the words, "Will the defendant please rise?" he got to his feet, his lawyer standing beside him.

"Members of the jury, have you reached a verdict?" asked Judge Walters.

The jury spokesman stood, staring directly at the judge and avoiding making any eye contact with the defendant whatsoever. "Yes, your honour, we have. The members of this jury find the defendant Mr Max Davies *guilty.*"

Max's stomach dropped. Had he heard that right?

"Members of the jury," Judge Eric Walters said, "this court dismisses you and thanks you. Mr Max Davies, I sentence you to a minimum of fifteen years in Her Majesty's Prison. Court is adjourned."

The Bailiff stood then, announcing, "All rise!" in his loud, booming voice.

Everyone in the courtroom stood, and after Judge Eric Walters had left the bench, Max was taken straight out of the courtroom to the cells. As he walked he looked shell-shocked, a scared, broken man.

Lauren was aware that people in the courtroom were staring at her. What she hadn't been aware of was that she'd been shouting at the jury – if she didn't stop she would soon be in contempt of court.

Before Lauren could say anything else Chloe ushered her out through the oak double doors, and for a while they just sat outside the courtroom so Lauren could regain her composure. Once Lauren's breathing had regulated, Chloe spoke to her.

"You need to stay in the moment, Lauren, not look beyond that," she suggested, unsure how she could possibly make Lauren feel any better.

"I still want Max in my life."

"You need to take it one day at a time."

"It hurts so much. I love him."

Chloe frowned. "Are you sure? I mean, you haven't been with him that long."

"Yes," said Lauren, nodding, "I've never been so sure about anything. I'm going to see him through this. I'm going to arrange a visit straight away." She began to sob again.

Chloe reached for a tissue from her bag. "Here, shall I ring your mother?"

"No," Lauren said as she wiped her eyes, "I don't want her to know; she won't understand." Lauren hadn't disclosed any information to her mother about Max – other than that he was her new boyfriend – and she was glad of that now.

Knowing that she had to get herself under control, Lauren closed her eyes, breathing in for the count of four, and then breathing out for the count of four. She did this until she was calm.

"Let's go for a coffee," Chloe suggested. "We can have a proper chat and figure out what you're going to do. Come on, let's get out of here." Standing up, she took Lauren's arm.

As they stepped outside the court, the grey skies opened and a deluge of rain hammered down on them. Making a run for it, they headed to the nearest coffee shop, situated just around the corner. Although it was packed with people sheltering from the rain, Chloe managed to nab a stool at the back, offering it to Lauren while she ordered the coffees.

Lauren felt cold and dizzy, and her hands were shaking. She felt ill, but she knew it was probably just the shock of Max going to prison.

"You okay, Lauren?" Chloe asked as she placed the coffees down on the table. "Your skin's gone grey." Putting her arm around Lauren, she gave her a tight squeeze.

"I have to admit, I do feel a bit odd," came Lauren's shaky reply.

"Here, have a sip of this." Chloe handed her the mug. "There's plenty of sugar in it."

Lauren gulped a few mouthfuls and then looked down at the floor. "I feel so guilty."

"Whatever for?"

"My testimony didn't help Max at all. I completely lost it out there; the jury must have thought I was a mad woman."

"Stop right there," Chloe said, putting on her stern voice. "You did amazing in court – you should be proud of yourself."

"But he's gone to prison for something he didn't do!" Lauren wailed. "I know he didn't do it."

"Lauren," said Chloe, softening her voice now, "you should think long and hard about why you want a relationship with Max. Is it really love? Or is it just because you're lonely?" Chloe knew she was being tough, but she only wanted the best for her friend.

"I *do* love him and he loves me!" Lauren said, sounding adamant. "You can fall in love at first sight, you know – just because it took you six years doesn't mean we all take that long."

"Wow, that was below the belt."

"Sorry," Lauren sighed. "I didn't mean it."

"Yes, you did. Look, Lauren, I only want what's best for you. If you love Max like you say you do I will do everything I can to support you."

Chloe gave Lauren a huge smile, and for the first time that day Lauren felt ever so slightly better.

Chapter Eleven

It took sixty days for Lauren to get approved for a visit to see Max in prison, and when she did the list of don'ts was endless: no yoga pants, no sleeveless tops, no open-toed shoes, nothing tight or low-cut, no colours like the inmates wear, no underwire bras.

Lauren couldn't wait to see Max; although she was apprehensive about walking into this prison for the first time, she wanted to do it. After all, she would do anything to see him.

As she spied the facility on the horizon, she realised she felt oddly different to the times she'd visited Max on remand – this seemed far more… real. The notorious military prison seemed to have been made to look as gloomy as possible. There was no beauty in its design at all – only brutal efficiency – and there were no colours in sight, except for the red warning siren. As she drove towards it, its thirteen-foot-high gate – a grey mass of steel beams and wire – loomed up in front of her.

Once she was inside, Lauren nervously waited until she was called, but once the process had started, she felt a little better; a thrill of excitement ran through her as she walked through a metal detector and had her hand stamped with ink – ink that was invisible to the naked eye but that would show up under a lamp. Security would check her hand on exit. Lauren had been given a pass to go to the visiting room, and after holding up the pass to the security guards on the other side of the door, she was buzzed in.

Cautiously, she entered the room, the security guard inside letting her know her seat assignment. There were tables lined up along the room, the inmates sitting in plastic chairs while they awaited their visitors. Empty chairs were placed opposite them. Lauren followed the leader, an older woman who looked like she'd lived a hard life. This woman walked straight over to an aged inmate and kissed him on both cheeks.

As Lauren looked around the room, she couldn't help but shudder. She just hated the eerie atmosphere that seemed to linger in the air, and she couldn't help but wonder if it felt like this every day in this cold, sombre building. Did the inmates feel it too? The visitors? The guards?

Then she saw him: Max was sitting at the last table in the room, staring at her and smiling. Lauren walked over, and as she pulled the chair out from under the table, she smiled back. She felt awkward, and flustered, like she didn't know what to do. Should she kiss Max? Hug him? Or at least do something? Why did everything feel so strange? When Max touched her hand for a brief moment, however, relief flooded Lauren's heart.

"Thanks for coming," said Max.

"You know I wouldn't miss it," Lauren replied, still feeling slightly awkward. "I just wish I could have come sooner."

Lauren was glad to see Max after all this time, but the prison officers who were patrolling the room with such vigour and intensity made her feel uncomfortable. She desperately wanted to say what she'd come here to say, but it was almost like the officers were listening in. She wanted to remain upbeat for Max's sake but it was hard – she'd never lived through anything like this before.

Ten minutes of polite conversation passed by before she blurted it out. "Max, I've made a decision: I'm going to campaign to get you released." Lauren was aware that she'd be raising Max's hopes, but if she was going to get him released she needed him to understand and fully cooperate.

"And how are you going to do that, Lauren?" he asked, his expression unchanging.

"The police tricked you into a confession," she said simply, "they can't do that."

"They didn't trick me, Lauren – I said those words myself."

"Okay, but they coerced you into it, didn't they? I'm serious, Max. I'm going to get you out of here. You can't stay here; you've got to fight, so we can be together." A tear escaped Lauren's eye and Max wiped it away with his thumb. A prison officer immediately walked to their table, giving them both a long, menacing stare. Clearly, touching wasn't allowed.

"Oh Lauren, don't be upset," Max said once the officer had walked off again. "You have to be realistic. I'm not going to get released, but... will you wait for me, my sweet? Please wait for me. I want us to be together more than anything. I know it's a big ask, but we're meant to be together, I just know it."

Lauren sniffed. "Of course I will, Max, but please believe me: I'm going to get you released. I have a meeting with one of the best defence lawyers in the country tomorrow. I need you to meet him too."

Max sighed. "If that's what you want, my sweet, I will."

Soon it was time to leave, the hour having vanished so quickly, and Lauren was delighted that she'd managed to turn Max around: he believed she'd meant every word. After an emotional goodbye, Lauren turned to see Max being escorted out of the visiting room. She blew a kiss his way, and just before he vanished out of sight, he winked at her.

Once he was out of the room, he smiled to himself, surprised that his plan was beginning to work. His eyes grew big as he visualised the future, when Lauren would be all his.

Chapter Twelve

The very next day Lauren found herself sitting opposite defence lawyer Curtis Rowland, feeling quite anxious. He was renowned for his straight-talking attitude and his ability to get stuff done, and she really didn't know what she'd do if he chose not to represent Max – first, he had to read the account of the criminal investigation into Max's case.

As Curtis read the paperwork he made soft humming noises, tapping his fingers on his desk and occasionally raising his eyebrows. Lauren looked around his office; she thought it would be more modern going by its exterior; the elaborate white stone single-storey office looked out of place in the poverty-stricken area, and while the office itself was adorned with old-fashioned furniture that was surely expensive, it wasn't to Lauren's liking at all. Aluminium blinds covered the Vortex windows, while a mahogany sideboard in need of refurbishment stood erect in the corner.

"You like what you see, Ms Adams?" he asked, his eyes still glued to the papers in front of him.

"Um, it's different."

"Not to your taste then." Curtis stood up, closed the folder, and tossed it onto the desk. "Okay, Ms Adams."

"Please, call me Lauren."

"Well, Lauren, I've studied the case, and as far as I'm concerned you have a good chance of winning. It looks like they had insufficient evidence."

"Insufficient evidence? What do you mean?" Lauren asked, frowning in confusion.

"There's not enough evidence to suggest that Mr Davies used the knife to kill Thomas Victor. Yes, his fingerprints were found on the weapon, but it's inconclusive as to whether he actually committed the crime. No witnesses have come forward to prove this so the verdict was based on circumstantial evidence and circumstantial evidence alone."

"What about his confession?"

"We can work around that," Curtis replied, a twinkle in his eye. He sure did love a challenge.

"I see, so does this mean Max will be released?" Lauren stared at Curtis intently, hoping against hope he was going to say yes.

"I can't guarantee it, but he has a chance."

Lauren jumped up from her seat, shouting, "Yes!" before kissing Curtis Rowland on the cheek.

He stared at her, clearly astounded.

"Sorry, I got carried away!" she exclaimed. "Thank you, Mr Rowland, thank you so much."

"Thank me when we win." Curtis smiled at her. "I think Mr Max Davies is a very lucky man."

Feeling suddenly embarrassed but not wanting to show it, Lauren quickly asked, "So, what's next?"

"Well," said Curtis, "you usually only get one chance to appeal, so we must be on point. First off, I need to ask for the judge's permission to appeal against their decision, which is when I'll outline why the guilty verdict was wrong. This will probably take a couple of weeks. Once they give permission, we'll be granted a retrial."

"A couple of weeks, great. I can't wait to let Max know!"

Curtis held his hands up in front of him. "Let's not get carried away yet – it's important not to get his hopes up – but by all means let him know. This will give him something to focus on. I will contact you as soon as we have a date for the retrial."

Lauren nodded. "Thank you again, Mr Rowland."

"Curtis, please."

Lauren shook his hand gratefully, and Curtis showed her to the door. "Until next time, Lauren."

"Goodbye Curtis," Lauren said, and as she skipped out the door she shouted, "Thank you!"

*****

Curtis had only spent an hour with Max and already he was having doubts about him, but he knew it was vital to ignore his negative feelings towards his new client; he needed to remain professional and find the good in Max, allowing the relationship between them to grow.

After listening to Max disclose his account of what had happened, Curtis chose to follow the rule of innocent until proven guilty. Yes, he would represent Max, but those dubious thoughts still lingered.

Still, he wasn't getting paid to convict the man – he was getting paid to free him, no matter what.

*****

Smiling widely, Lauren read the front page of the tabloid newspaper again:

Max Davies, who was accused of murdering fifty-nine-year-old Thomas Victor, an insurance broker, has walked free from court after a jury failed to reach a verdict. Max Davies' fingerprints were found on the murder weapon but there was no sufficient evidence that he used the knife to kill the victim.

Judge Eric Walters ruled: "It would be unjust and despotic for the defendant Max Davies to be imprisoned any longer without sufficient evidence."

The case was acquitted.

It was the happiest day of Lauren's life.

Chapter Thirteen

Three years ago

Fairfax Financial was a financial holding company based in Toronto, Canada that engaged in property, casualty and investment insurance, claims, and investment management.

Jacob Adams was in his third year of being an employee, and after several small promotions he was slowly working his way to the top. His life in Canada was idyllic. Although he missed his family – especially Lauren – he rather liked being a loner. In the three years he'd been living in Canada he'd only returned to England once, and that was when his father had died.

Jacob had known Max Davies was trouble from day one, and his obsession with the man showed no signs of stopping. Ever since the time Jacob had viewed the open folder on Max's desk, revealing his secret, Jacob knew what he had to do: gather as much information on Max Davies as possible and report him to the CEO of Fairfax Financial.

Jacob had been playing a game with Max, causing the phrase *'treat me like a game and I'll show you how it's played'* to keep resurfacing in his brain. It was a source of fun and, overall, a challenge. As Max Davies responded to Jacob's strategy, they started to get along well. Max had no reason not to trust Jacob, and while he usually kept himself guarded against friendships as a rule, this time it was different. Max liked Jacob, but he knew he shouldn't get too close to him, especially as he was continuing to be a fraudulent friend. Soon he would have enough money in his Swiss bank account to retire on, and this time next year he'd be celebrating his birthday in Hawaii.

Jacob looked at the stack of red folders resting in his arms, hoping he was doing the right thing. One thing, however, was certain: there was no doubt in his mind of what Max Davies was up to.

He knocked gently on Mark Higgins' door. His appointment was for nine-thirty, and as usual, he was two minutes early – one of the superstitions he had regarding any important meeting. Jacob had made sure he was well prepared. After all, he knew he couldn't waste Mark Higgins' time; it was far too precious.

"Come in."

Jacob manoeuvred the folders, resting them on the inside of his elbow as he opened the door.

"Jacob, please." Mark Higgins gestured with his hand for him to sit down. "What can I do for you?"

Jacob sat down, placing the folders on Higgins' oak desk. Although an antique, with its dark brown colour and with no marks on it whatsoever, it looked brand new. It was a large piece of furniture that could accommodate ten people at a time, and consequently, it was where Mark held all his meetings. The conference room was painted in a nice light blue, evoking a relaxed and agreeable atmosphere. Blinds covered every window, obscuring the glare from outside.

Mark Higgins was a handsome fifty-three-year-old, the slight greying of hair around his temples the only thing giving away his age. He was at least six-feet tall, with an angular, slightly lined face, and he was always dressed in a navy blue off-the-peg suit with designer shoes, exuding flair and style. Mark was seen as a fair CEO, his responsibilities on the day-to-day management of Fairfax Financial being implemented with great dedication and passion. His corporate decisions surpassed most people's expectations. Jacob both liked and respected him.

"Well," said Jacob, adjusting his chair so he was at equal height, "it's about Max."

As Jacob talked Mark listened to him intently, his astonishment showing every so often in his body language and facial expressions.

When Jacob had finished what he'd come to say, Mark reclined backwards in his chair, scratching the side of his head. "Thank you for bringing this to light, Jacob," he said eventually. "I'm glad you didn't confront Max about his fraudulent acts yourself – coming to see me was the smart thing to do."

Jacob nodded. "I'd had my suspicions about him from day one, Mark. And now I know for sure – he's been draining the company of money to have the lifestyle he's become accustomed to."

"It looks like he's gathered together a substantial amount of money," Mark agreed.

"So what do you think you'll do, press charges?" asked Jacob, raising his eyebrows.

Mark thought about this for a moment. "I'll mull it over, but one thing's for sure: Max Davies won't be working for Fairfax Financial any longer. Would you do the honours of sending him up to me?"

"With pleasure."

Mark stood up and shook Jacob's hand. "I think you're due a promotion soon, Jacob."

"Oh," said Jacob as he stood up, "I didn't disclose this to gain anything; I just don't like dishonesty."

Mark nodded. "I like a man with high morals – you deserve to be rewarded. Well done, Jacob, you have the makings of a great project manager."

Jacob couldn't help but show his delight; his beaming smile, filled with genuineness, made his eyes crinkle. "Thank you, Mark. I won't let you down."

Back in the office, Jacob watched Max as he sat working at his desk. He was going to have great delight in sending him to Mark's office – it would be like an animal going to the slaughter.

He walked over to Max, standing tall with his shoulders pulled back as he said, "Mark would like to see you in his office." Jacob used his usual tone of voice – he didn't want to ignite any suspicion.

A grin immediately appeared on Max's face. "That must be for my promotion. He doesn't usually ask for anyone to see him in his office unless it's something important. What do you think, Jacob?"

"I have no idea."

Max got to his feet, whistling as he passed Jacob.

"Good luck," said Jacob with a smile.

"I won't need it," replied Max.

"Oh yes you will," Jacob muttered under his breath.

*****

Max knocked on Mark Higgins' door with confidence, and when he entered the office it was with a carefree attitude.

Mark didn't stand up to greet him, instead pointing to the chair and signalling for Max to sit. "I'm going to get straight to the point," Mark said, a serious expression on his face. "Max, I have evidence that you've been caught in a fraudulent act. Is this true?" He paused for a moment, looking him straight in the eye. "Your unwillingness to come forward and admit to this will only cause more damage."

This statement threw Max off balance, and he had to think quickly to reply. He noticed the red folders open on Mark's desk. "I don't understand," was all he could come up with.

"I would appreciate it if you were honest in this matter," said Mark, "and own up to any misconduct."

Max couldn't believe what he was hearing. How did he know? "Why would I steal from you?" he sneered. "Do I seem like the kind of person who would do something like that?"

"In one word – yes," Mark replied, his gaze never faltering.

"Don't you think somebody would have to be pretty stupid to do that?" Max asked, wriggling uneasily in his chair.

"Yes, I do," Mark replied. "This company has been good to you, so why did you do this? Tell me why!"

"But I haven't done anything!" Max protested. "This is absurd."

Mark threw the red folders across the desk. "Why don't you take a look?"

Max had no doubt in his mind that he'd been caught, but he was going to plead his innocence for as long as he could. Keeping silent, he picked up one red folder and then another. It was all there in black and white. It was no good: he'd been caught completely red-handed.

"Your contract will be terminated," Mark told him. "As I'm sure you can understand, I can't afford to give employees who commit fraud a second chance, nor would I want to."

"You can't do this," Max complained, "you can't fire me!"

Max leaned forwards, looking straight into his eyes as he said, "You should be grateful I'm not on the phone to the police right now. Go and clear your desk – I want you out of my sight."

Max said nothing as he silently stood and left the room.

Chapter Fourteen

Lauren couldn't thank Curtis Rowland enough. Although a big chunk of her inheritance had been blown on hiring him, it was well worth it; he'd done an upstanding job running circles around the prosecution.

"You were amazing, Curtis."

"Well, that's what you paid me to do," he replied, "but thank you."

"I'm so glad I had you representing Max," Lauren continued. "I didn't have any doubts, you know. I knew you'd do it."

"I knew too. Have a great life with Max, Lauren."

"I will – thanks to you." She walked over to him, kissing him on both cheeks, and as she watched him leave the court she wondered if he had someone to go home to. She hoped he did.

Lauren waited excitedly outside the courthouse, feeling great in her turquoise maxi dress that she'd bought especially for today. The weight loss over the last stressful months of Max's appeal had left her with a body she'd been striving for all her adult life, and the dress really accentuated her slimmer figure.

The court didn't look so grey and sombre to her anymore; what had once been an isolated, depressing vision was now a feature of positivity. While she waited, she took a moment to think back over the past few months. The campaign she'd embarked on to get Max released had completely taken over her life; the twelve hours a day she'd spent sifting through files and previous court cases had turned her into a recluse. During her crusade, losing touch with her dear friends had been the hardest brunt to bear, and it would be the first thing she'd put right once she was settled with Max.

Yes, her friends would be a big part of her life once again – if they wanted to, that was. Lauren knew Chloe was against her relationship with Max, as she'd advised her not to go ahead with the campaign. He'd been a virtual stranger back then, and Chloe had her reservations as to whether Max was telling the truth. What did Chloe think – that Lauren was having a relationship with a murderer? Once she got to know him well, her attitude towards him would change, Lauren was sure.

The court's front doors opened then and Lauren turned to look, hoping for Max. Instead, an old man with tattoos covering his neck and arms made his way through the doors. He was met by a younger man, and when they embraced the old man whispered something into the young man's ear. He smiled, grabbed the old man's holdall, and slung it into a nearby white transit van. He then tossed the keys to the old man to catch. Lauren watched the excitement grow on the old man's face as he climbed into the driver's side of the van. The engine started and they slowly pulled away.

Lauren wondered if it would take them long to re-establish their relationship. He'd obviously just had his case overturned and had probably been away from his family for months, even years. Although Max hadn't been away for years, Lauren still had concerns as to how long it would take her and Max to settle down into a normal life. After the busy campaign and the excitement of Max's release, she thought it would take quite a while.

When the sun made a brief appearance, breaking through the patchy cloud above, there he was: Max was in the outside world once again.

Lauren didn't know whether to run up to him or wait for him to walk up to her; after hesitating for a moment, she didn't delay any longer, sprinting towards him and kissing him passionately on the lips. His response was unimaginable – so gentle and yet so passionate. In that moment, she knew this was where she belonged, right here in Max's arms.

"Well, aren't you a sight to behold?" Max asked, holding her hands and squeezing them tightly.

"I love you," Lauren replied quickly, her eyes lingering on his.

"I love you too," Max replied, smiling. "Now, can we get going, sweet? I want to get as far away from this place as quickly as I can."

"Yes, sorry. You don't want to be hanging around here any more than you have to." Lauren bent down to seize the holdall Max had been carrying. It was identical to the one the old man had.

"No!"

Lauren jumped as Max tore the holdall away from her, his raised voice seeming to echo all around her.

"I'll carry it, sweetheart," he added, his voice having quickly returned to the pleasant tone he usually used. "I just don't want you struggling."

Lauren frowned, sensing that Max was on edge, but then again what had she expected? After all he'd been through, his nerves were surely in tatters.

"Okay, do you want to drive, Max?" Lauren asked, remembering the excitement on the old man's face as he'd driven away.

"Why would I want to do that?"

"Sorry, Max, I just thought…"

"Well, you were wrong," he replied, sighing loudly. "For god's sake, Lauren, what's wrong with you?"

"What's wrong with me?" Lauren asked, surprised. "Are you feeling alright, Max?" She stared at him, waiting for an answer, but he didn't give her one.

They got into the car in silence, the whole journey to the rented house carried out in a complete absence of sound. Lauren tried to remain calm, and though she was determined not to cry, it was hard. This wasn't the homecoming she'd dreamed of at all.

The furnished two-bedroomed detached house in the village of Heptonstall looked inviting with its bright cream exterior and large windows. It was the sort of house that gave you warm feelings as you entered it; there were several cosy rooms to relax in, and that's exactly what Lauren had wanted.

In the lounge, the grey chintz sofa went well with the salmon pink walls and the white flecked marble that surrounded the enormous fireplace. A Himalayan salt lamp sat alone on the stone hearth; salt lamps were used for healing and Max needed that. The small open kitchen revealed black granite worktops with wooden units. The white ceramic sink was less modern; it was almost out of sync with the rest of the house. Alongside the kitchen, a staircase led to a basement – the only room Lauren didn't like. There appeared to be an odd atmosphere in there, and as there were no windows to let fresh air through, the musky aroma had hit her nostrils immediately when she'd first set foot in there. Max had insisted on a basement, though, as he needed one to turn into a gym – he wanted to work out every day. Even with attending gym sessions in prison, he'd lost his muscular build. Anyway, he was welcome to the basement – she wasn't intending to enter it anytime soon. Upstairs there were two large identical bedrooms, both featuring green embossed wallpaper and matching throws on the beds. A white sparkling bathroom was a tad small but quaint. The house had the added bonus of a double garage, which would only be used as a storage room. The area was surrounded by green fields, so there'd be no nosy neighbours prying into their lives.

When he was in prison, Max had advised Lauren on the kind of house he wanted to share with her: it had to be a peaceful and comfortable place to live. Lauren had carefully scoured the area to find this idyllic location, about forty minutes on the train or a one-hour-twenty-minute drive from Manchester. She thought it was perfect.

As they stood together on the doorstep of the new rented house, Lauren placed the key in the lock and opened the front door. Turning around to Max she said, "Welcome home," and kissed him on the cheek.

"Home – what a sublime word," replied Max. "Thank you, Lauren, this house looks perfect."

"Wait until you see inside. Come on." Excited, Lauren grabbed Max's hand and led the way.

After getting a quick tour from Lauren, Max agreed that the house was ideal – she'd done a great job finding it.

Finally, all the planning he'd done in prison was working out – what he hadn't expected was to be released so quickly. As he stood at the top of the basement steps Max envisaged what he could do with it.

He could sound-proof it and make it impossible to escape from.

He had the skills. And he knew just the person to put in there.

Chapter Fifteen

As the morning sunshine cast shadows on the bedroom curtains, Lauren glanced across at the clock, which was perched precariously on the edge of the bedside cabinet. She moved it to the centre. Seven forty-five.

Max was still asleep, his face buried in the pillow. The connection between them last night had been electric; never before had she experienced a union like she'd had with Max. Their lovemaking had been intense, sweet, and passionate.

The pleased look on Lauren's face expanded as Max woke and propped himself up on the pillow.

"Morning, sweet."

"Morning! Would you like breakfast?"

"If it's you, then yes," he replied.

Lauren snuggled into Max as they picked up where they'd left off last night.

An hour later, Lauren was busy in the kitchen preparing a late breakfast of eggs benedict, Max's favourite. There were still so many facts she didn't know about Max, but she'd certainly have fun finding out. She wanted to know all his favourite things so she could make him happy.

As she set the scene for an intimate breakfast, Lauren realised she hadn't seen or heard from Max for at least thirty minutes. She searched the entire house calling his name, but there was no answer. The only room she hadn't checked was the basement.

As she turned the handle to the door, a strange feeling surfaced inside her, and she shook her shoulders to rid herself of the uncomfortable sensation. She tried the basement door again, but it wouldn't open – it must be locked. How could that be? She tried it a third time, and she was just about to walk away when it opened. Max was standing there in his gym shorts, his torso dripping with beads of sweat.

"Max, you scared me."

"Sorry sweet. What are you doing snooping around here anyway?"

"I wasn't snooping; I was looking for you. Breakfast is ready."

"I don't want you anywhere near the basement – you hear me, Lauren?"

"Yes, yes, I hear you." Lauren stomped back to the kitchen, wondering what was wrong with Max as she ate her breakfast alone. Yes, he'd only just been released from prison and therefore had to adapt again to civilisation, but she hadn't expected him to be so moody, snapping at everything she did or said. What was he doing down the basement anyway?

Just then she heard footsteps approach, and when she looked up she saw Max standing in the doorway of the kitchen.

"Eating alone, Lauren? We can't have that." He pulled a chair out from under the kitchen table and sat down.

"It's cold now – I'll make you some more. It's your favourite." Lauren got up, removing the plate that was in front of him.

"Stop." Max grabbed her arm, taking the plate away from her with his free hand. "It will be fine; for months I've been used to having it like that. Sit down, Lauren."

As Lauren sat down, tears began to well in her eyes. She tried – and failed – to hide her face.

"Look, Lauren," Max sighed, "I'm sorry I've been tough on you, but I need my own space. The basement will be my retreat, where I can reflect and work out how to keep my sanity. I don't want you anywhere near my space – the basement is out of bounds, okay sweet?"

Lauren looked up at Max. His face appeared angry through the fake smile he showed her.

"I understand," she said eventually, "but what were you doing down there? We haven't bought any workout equipment yet." As she spoke she noticed some dirt ingrained in his fingernails and fresh black earth on his brow.

"I don't need all that equipment – although I will need a treadmill and some monkey bars and rope to get started. It's very dirty down there, Lauren, look." Max turned his palms upwards, revealing the dirt and grime Lauren had noticed only a second ago. "It's just really dirty; you wouldn't want to go down there anyway."

Lauren nodded.

Max tucked into his cold breakfast as silence fell in the room. Minutes passed before he spoke again. "So, what are we going to do today, sweet?"

"I thought I'd go and see Chloe, give you the space you probably need," Lauren said, knowing she was being sarcastic but unable to stop herself.

"No! You don't have to do that. We'll spend the day together. How about we go for a walk in all that open greenery?" Max nodded towards the kitchen window.

"That will be lovely," Lauren agreed. She was glad she hadn't arranged anything with Chloe – if she had and then cancelled, she would've felt embarrassed. She would arrange a night out with her soon.

*****

Lauren and Max spent a lovely afternoon together, walking in the beautiful green countryside; it reminded Lauren of the delightful cottage she grew up in. Nothing could beat the open space surrounding them, especially the fields of green and yellow cowslips that lined up in a stripe formation. The occasional nod to passers-by made them feel like part of the community. They must've walked for miles and talked for hours.

By the end of their walk Lauren was feeling optimistic about the future; she felt sure they'd be happy living here in the countryside.

They stopped off at the local pub for a thirst-quenching aperitif before heading home, where Max was going to cook dinner. A visit to the local farm shop enticed them into buying organic produce.

"My speciality steak in pepper sauce, seasonal vegetables, and home-made mashed potato are to die for, Lauren," Max whispered.

"I can't wait," she laughed in response. She couldn't help noticing the cashier smiling at them – she was probably thinking, 'what a lovely young couple in love'.

Lauren sighed in contentment. The feelings she had for Max were unique, new, and marvellous, and she knew Max felt the same.

Chapter Sixteen

Having lived together now for six months, Lauren couldn't believe how happy she was. Her relationship with Max had grown into a really strong, solid one, and it was so exciting, learning everything there was to learn about each other.

There was food for thought in many areas, such as: what was she to do with her rented flat? After all, the lease was nearly up. And when was she going to return to work? The head, Chris Edwards, had been so accommodating with the amount of time she'd had off but she was missing it, and the children.

When she made the suggestion to Max, however, he bluntly refused; he didn't want her to return to work, not now, not ever. "No girlfriend of mine is going to work for a living," he told her. "It's as simple as that."

Lauren was astonished at his reaction, but instead of getting into an argument about it, she decided to leave it for now and try to discuss it again another time.

To celebrate their six-month anniversary, Lauren decided to surprise Max with a gift, cementing her love for him. This gift would be special, and personal, and forever.

As she sat in the tattooist's chair, Lauren admired the artwork pinned on the walls: large images of bright colours etched on all different shades of skin. How creative these artists were.

"All ready, Miss?" asked Tex.

Tex the tattooist had a large following; he was renowned in the area for his amazing artwork. After Aaron, Chloe's husband, had recommended him to her, Lauren had gone and booked her appointment straight away. Aaron couldn't praise Tex enough, though he'd reminded Lauren that Chloe was missing her, and he'd made her promise to see her soon. Lauren felt awful for neglecting her (and the rest of her friends), but she would soon put it right. Before she'd left, she'd made Aaron promise not to tell Chloe about the conversation they'd had. She knew Chloe would've tried talking her out of having a tattoo – she detested them on women.

Lauren looked at Tex's forearm, which was covered by a beautiful tattoo of a woman with a dove on her head. It was so striking, Lauren wondered who she was. In a weird sort of way she found Tex handsome, even though he had an unkempt look about him. His long, dull black hair had grease at the roots, and his distinguished goatee beard looked like it hadn't been washed for a while. Even so, he had magnetic eyes that drew you to him.

"Yep, I'm ready."

As the needle touched her skin Lauren gasped, expecting pain, but all she felt was a vague tingle. She'd made a basic sketch of what she wanted the tattoo to look like, and had decided where it would go, but it was Tex who had made sure the tattoo design looked perfect and unique. She couldn't wait to see the finished product, and she wasn't disappointed.

As she admired her new – and first – tattoo, she knew Max would love it. She couldn't wait to show it off to him.

*****

Gaily walking through the front door, Lauren kicked her shoes off, placing them neatly at the bottom of the stairs. Max hated the way her shoes were always strewn all over the place – by the front door, by the bed, by the sofa – so now she had a habit of arranging them precisely, just to please him.

Max was lying on the sofa, watching TV, and as she looked at him she couldn't help but feel full of desire; her attraction for him never seemed to weaken. Tip-toeing towards him, she lunged at him, making him jump.

Max froze, the hairs on the back of his neck standing on end. "For Christ's sake, Lauren!" he yelled.

"Sorry! I didn't mean to scare you!"

"Why would you do that?" Max's face was ashen as he pushed Lauren aside and stood up. "Where have you been anyway?"

"I'm really sorry, Max," Lauren said quietly, thinking that she'd probably spoilt the moment now.

"So you bloody should be! Don't ever do that again."

"I've got a surprise for you, babe," she said, trying to lighten the mood. "But first, wait here." She went to the kitchen and opened the bottle of champagne that had been chilling in the fridge; she'd placed it there that morning to go with her surprise. She poured the champagne into two crystal champagne flutes that she'd had engraved with the words, 'Happy six-month anniversary'. Then, carrying a silver tray with a candle set in between the glasses, she walked into the lounge, switching the main room light off to set the mood.

"Happy six-month anniversary, love!" she exclaimed.

"Oh, Lauren, you're so sweet."

"Here, take one," Lauren said, offering the tray to Max. "Cheers!"

"Cheers." Max pecked Lauren on the cheek.

"That's not all," she said, placing the tray and glass down on the corner table. "Look what I had done today!" Grinning,

101

Lauren displayed the fire tattoo she'd got on the inside of her wrist.

Max didn't speak – he just stared at the black ink as his face turned red with anger.

*****

Lauren looked in the bathroom mirror, cringing at the sight of her face. How was she going to leave the house with a black, swollen eye?

She remembered the rasp of Max's breathing as he hit her, his face contorting into a beast-like expression, his eyes watery and his veins standing out.

She shook herself to get rid of the memory, then looked down at the plaster covering her wrist – Max had made her wear it to cover up the tattoo. He didn't ever want to see it again. It wasn't her fault; she hadn't realised Max's fire tattoo represented an unpleasant time in his life. How was she to know if he'd never told her about it? At least applying make-up to the bruise had covered it reasonably well.

Lauren hadn't seen Max all night, and in the morning he'd been busy in the basement. He could remain there, for all she cared. The tapping sound coming from the basement hadn't stopped all night, and Lauren had no idea what Max was doing. The dreaded noise had kept her awake – not that she would've been able to sleep after being hit in the face by his brutal fist.

Lauren thought back to their confrontation, a fresh wave of humiliation washing over her. Would she be able to forgive and forget? She knew she had to learn to resolve conflict instead of walking away like she usually did, but she also didn't want to engage with him again for quite some time. A cooling off period was what she needed, some alone time in order to process her thoughts and feelings. She would come back to Max with a clearer head and a more open heart.

Once she was ready, she left the house to go for a peaceful walk in the countryside. The fresh air was blowing and she admired the dense green crops as she carried herself through the open space. After walking for a couple of miles, the pain in her heart began to ease. Images of the hatred showing in Max's eyes kept returning, however, and she knew she needed to clear the air with him – otherwise they'd never move on. His emotions had been running high last night and they needed to make up in order to release some of the built-up tension. He would never hit her again. She wouldn't allow it.

The more she thought about it, the more shocked she was at his outburst; perhaps he'd been harbouring this dark secret inside him for many years.

Suddenly feeling cold and tired, Lauren pulled the collar of her jacket up around her neck as she walked briskly back to the house, glad of a clearer head. Now she just wanted to confront Max and put the fight behind them.

When she got in the first thing she saw, on the kitchen table, was a handwritten card expressing his apologies lying next to a huge bouquet of flowers. Max had made the first move of a peace offering.

"Arguments happen even in the strongest, happiest relationships, Lauren," Max said as he walked into the kitchen. "I regret what happened, and I love you so much. I'm so sorry about the fight."

"You hurt me, Max," Lauren replied quietly, "and not just on the outside."

"Please help me understand what you're feeling." He held his hand open, gesturing for Lauren to sit down. He was giving her his full attention.

"What made you do it?" she asked as she sat, her voice shaking slightly.

"I'm sorry for fighting with you," he said in response, "and I know that my behaviour needs to change. It's just about what happened in my past. Are you willing to listen?"

Lauren nodded. "I'm ready." She placed her elbows on the table, resting her chin on the knuckles of her hands.

Max sat down opposite her. "My dear old mother died in a house fire, and it took me a long time to recover from it. I was only twelve years old." His voice cracked on the last word and he began to weep.

"Oh, I'm so sorry, Max, I really am," Lauren said, "but how does this relate to your outburst last night?"

"This." Max pointed to the small fire tattoo on his neck.

Lauren frowned. "I don't understand."

"This tattoo is a testament to my mother, and when I saw the same one on your wrist it took me back to a place I haven't revisited for a long time. My emotions escalated. I'm so sorry."

Lauren stood up and walked over to Max, cupping her arms around him. She didn't agree that this was a good enough reason for a fight, but now the reason had been addressed, Lauren recognised that holding onto her emotion of anger would not improve the situation for either of them.

Holding Max's hand, she led the way upstairs to the bedroom, allowing the relief of their reconciliation to spill over into a session of romantic reunion that reaffirmed the bond of love between them.

Max

Max stared at Lauren as she slept, her arm sprawled out above her head revealing the fire tattoo she'd uncovered from the plaster. He knew he'd done a good job – once again she'd fallen for his lies.

As he watched her, the anger started boiling up inside him, his response to her provocation.

It was time…

Chapter Seventeen

Finally, Lauren had got around to arranging a night out with Chloe – dinner then a few cocktails – and she hoped it would go well, as tonight she wanted to make a statement to Chloe. She wanted her friend to see how happy she was, how blissful her relationship with Max was turning out to be.

Max had gone out for a run like he often did, and on his return he would always head straight for the basement. Lauren was still intrigued as to what he got up to down there, especially as he didn't seem to be working out. There was a constant knocking and banging as if he was building something, but she never dared to ask.

She'd made the most of her time getting ready for tonight – her hair pinned up, her make-up immaculate – and once she was done she marvelled at herself in the mirror. The front door opened and then slammed shut. Max was home.

As she'd guessed he made his way straight to the basement, and a second later she heard the turn of the lock. It was nearly time to go, and she wanted to show Max how good she looked – she needed reassurance from him. So, pottering along in her high heels towards the basement, she called out to Max several times. No answer. She wondered for a moment if she should knock on the basement door, but not wanting to upset him, she decided against it. She'd send him a text later instead, when she was out. Lauren smiled as she took one last look in the hall mirror, then she grabbed her keys and closed the front door behind her.

The sleek cocktail lounge – with its art deco design and bespoke style – secreted an air of sophistication, offering guests a brilliant spot in which they could relax and unwind. Low lighting added to the feel of a chilled retreat. Lauren loved it. Chloe was already there to greet her, sitting at a cosy table at the back of the lounge with two strawberry margaritas in front of her, the delicious-looking drinks just waiting to be sipped. A perfect way to relax together and have a much-needed catch-up.

Lauren kissed Chloe on the cheek. "Hi babe, long time no see."

"Too right, you bloody loved-up recluse!" Chloe shot back.

"I'm sorry." Lauren gave her an apologetic smile.

"Only joking, I'm so happy for you. Here, drink this." Chloe handed her the cocktail.

Lauren sat down in the softly cushioned armchair opposite her friend, and as she sipped at her drink, she couldn't help but feel nostalgic – she'd forgotten how nice it was being with her.

"Come on then," said Chloe, "spill the beans!"

Lauren wondered how she knew; the bruise on her face had almost vanished. Her face drained of blood and she suddenly became panicky. "How do you know?"

"Know what?" Chloe stared at her, baffled.

"About Max."

"What about him? What are you talking about?"

Relief swept over Lauren as she realised Chloe didn't know. She thought quickly of something she could say. "That he doesn't want me to go back to work," she said after taking a long sip of her drink.

"Um – I didn't know that. I was just asking what you've been up to since I saw you last. Are you okay, Lauren?"

Lauren's phone beeped then, and removing it from her bag, she saw she had one unread message. It was from Max: *Get home now.*

Lauren chose to dismiss Max's request, though doing so put her on edge. She so wanted tonight to be special; she hadn't seen Chloe for so long.

"Are you sure you're okay, Lauren? Chloe asked again.

"I'm fine, why do you ask?" Lauren replied, trying to sound casual.

"You just seem a little… twitchy, almost like you're scared of something."

"Don't be silly, what have I got to be scared about? Oh! Guess what?"

"What?"

"I got a tattoo." Lauren turned her arm over, revealing the fire design on her wrist. "Wasn't I brave? It's identical to the one Max has on his neck."

"Um, that's… different."

"Don't you like it?"

Chloe frowned. "You must love Max very much; it's a pretty big thing to have done."

"That's right," said Lauren, a little defensively, "it's to cement our relationship."

"Right. Anyway, when are we going on another girly weekend?" Chloe asked, quickly changing the subject. "The girls have been asking after you. You don't seem to answer any of their calls?"

Lauren could tell Chloe was annoyed. "I'm not sure when I'll be able to do that," Lauren replied. "Max still doesn't like being on his own; I don't really want to leave him by himself just yet." She realised she sounded like she was under Max's thumb, the expression on Chloe's face telling her she thought the same.

As the night continued, Chloe noticed that Lauren was constantly watching the time – every so often her gaze would drift to the clock on the wall.

"Am I boring you?" Chloe asked eventually.

"No, of course not," Lauren replied, shaking her head. "To tell you the truth, I'm not feeling too great. Would you mind if we called it a night? Catch up another time?" she asked, almost pleading.

"Why didn't you say something earlier? You're not pregnant, are you?" giggled Chloe.

"No, nothing like that, I just think I'm getting a migraine." Lauren stood up, kissed Chloe goodbye, and then made a quick exit. She ran all the way to her car, ignoring people as they stared at her. Her face was red and sweaty, not from the running but from the fear she had of facing Max after defying him. That dreaded night when they'd had that fight was coming back to haunt her.

Back in the bar, Chloe was left feeling mystified. She sensed that Lauren was in some kind of danger, and while her sixth sense was usually right, she hoped – this time – it was wrong.

Climbing into Clara, Lauren clocked the time on the dashboard – it had been almost two hours since Max had sent the demanding text. Just how angry would he be? With trembling hands she put the key into the ignition, though it wasn't just her hands trembling but her whole body. As beads of sweat began to form on her forehead, she realised it was the start of a panic attack – she recognised the signs. She hadn't experienced anxiety since her mid-twenties, but she could always remember the start of an attack.

Concentrating on her breathing she tried to steady herself, placing her shaking hands on the steering wheel and taking deep, slow breaths. Soon enough she had her panic under control, and with haste she drove home.

Once she'd parked up outside the house she dashed out of the car, removing her heels and hotfooting it to the front door. As she put the key in the lock she half expected Max to be standing there, waiting for her, and for a split second she hated herself for being so weak, for not being able to do what she wanted. When had she become so timid?

Inside, she climbed the stairs, the imprint of her feet leaving an impression in the thick grey cable carpet. There was no sign of Max anywhere. Slipping off her red lacy dress, she changed into the lightweight blue camisole set she'd bought on impulse – she'd decided to treat herself. Perhaps it would treat Max too. Perhaps then he wouldn't be too upset with her.

Lauren crept downstairs heel first so she wouldn't make a noise, and then scoured the downstairs rooms one by one. Max was nowhere to be seen, and his shoes weren't by the front door – he must be out. She noticed a black key fob half hidden under the bread bin, and picking it up she read the white sticker attached to it – 'basement'. Dare she take a look? No. She placed it back down. Max had surely put it there for a reason. Maybe he'd been forgetful and careless by leaving it out for her to see. She reckoned the bread bin had been home to the key all along.

She stared at the suspicious key, lying there, staring up at her. This was her chance to see what Max had been up to. So, picking the key up, she started turning it over in her palms. Although she was eager to see the basement, she felt slightly apprehensive. What would she find?

As she made her way to the basement door she wondered if she should text Max – to see where he was and to find out what time he'd be home – but that would give her less time to view the basement, and she desperately wanted to do that. So, nervously, she put the key into the lock, turning it clockwise and then anti-clockwise. No joy. She tried again. Still no luck. If this key didn't belong to the basement door, where did it belong?

Lauren gave a big sigh, disappointed that she couldn't gain access. She returned to the kitchen to put the key back where it belonged, and when she raised the lid to the bread bin she saw three keys lying at the back, each one with the same label. *The larger of the keys is obviously the one to the basement door,* Lauren thought, *but what are the other two for?* They were both of a smaller size, almost like a handcuff key. She remembered when her brother Jacob had his sheriff's outfit for his eighth birthday; he repeatedly wanted to cuff her hands, pretending he was making an arrest – the memory brought a smile to her face. Slowly, she picked up the other keys, intrigued as to where they fit, and so – for the second time that evening – she started making her way to the basement.

As she put the larger key into the lock, her anticipation grew with the expectation of what was waiting for her on the other side. Turning the key, the sound of a metallic grind made her spine tingle, and twisting the handle, she gasped as the door creaked open.

She was welcomed by an eerie darkness, and in a burst of panic, she fumbled for the light switch. She flipped it up and down frantically, but the room remained immersed in darkness. How did Max work in this lack of light? Leaning against the cold stone bricks of the wall, she slowly inched herself down each step of the rickety stairs until she was at the bottom. The arid air and stench made her gasp, and as she put her hand to her mouth she dropped one of the keys. "Oh shit!" she cursed.

Sliding her foot along the ground, a feeling of wet earth raked between her toes. *"What the hell?"* she shouted, shocked and intrigued. The pitch-black room was beginning to swallow her up. She was being drawn in, like there was no escape. Putting one foot in front of the other, she made her way into the wide open space.

A few seconds later she heard a barely audible click coming from the door, as if someone had locked it on the outside, then the clunk of a key turning in a lock. Hoping she'd heard wrong, Lauren made her way slowly back up the steps, grabbing the door handle and trying to turn it. Someone had locked it.

Lauren froze for a moment, completely shocked, and then started twisting and shaking the doorknob, hoping it was just stuck. Banging the door and turning the handle, she tried to coax it open. Clearly, it wasn't going to budge.

"Max, Max please – open the door, Max!" she shouted as she kicked the door.

Why didn't she think to bring her phone? She always took her phone everywhere.

"Max, help me – please!"

As soon as Max was back, surely he'd hear her cries and open the door.

"Max, I'm in here! The door locked! I'm in the basement!" she screamed as loud as she could.

She knew she was becoming hysterical, and she also knew it wouldn't help things, but what else could she do?

Slowly, she sat down with her back against the door, lifting her legs up and cradling her knees with her arms. She was still holding on tightly to the two keys. How had she got herself into this mess? Being curious had always got her into trouble.

Her mother Nancy often told her she'd been born curious, always asking questions that started how, what, why, where, and when ever since the day she could talk. If she didn't have many surprises in her life, Lauren got bored and disengaged. Consequently, she took more risks in the hope of leading an exciting and full life. It didn't feel like that now; it felt like a life full of danger and confusion.

Sitting on her bottom, Lauren started easing herself down the steps, but it was so dark it was like she was blindfolded. She remembered the game she used to play with Jacob when they were young: he would blindfold her, spin her around, then go and hide. She'd have ten minutes to find him, and if she didn't, he would win. But this time it wasn't a game – this was real.

She knew it was important to stay calm, but the darkness and lack of fresh air made her heart race. As she crawled along to the centre of the room she could feel dirt coagulate under her fingernails, making her think back to the dirt she'd seen under Max's fingernails. She swallowed her own saliva, trying to reduce the thirst that was quickly growing in the back of her throat. The ominous feeling in the pit of her stomach wouldn't subside, and aware that she was growing weary, she made a last attempt to call for Max so he could free her. Feeling in front of her, she touched a wall, and standing rigid to the spot, she yelled, "Max, help me!" The sound of the resulting silence made her weep, but pulling herself together, she told herself not to give up. It was time to try the door again.

She walked up the steps one at a time, her arms balanced by her sides, the feeling of unsteadiness making her cautious. She took another shaky step, then another, then another, until she reached the top, the last step creaking and moaning under her feet. Her body stiffened as she imagined herself plummeting downwards. She pounded on the door, making her knuckles sore, her head throbbing from the noise of her desperate calls for help and her bare feet aching from the constant kicking on the door. Feeling scared and lonely, she willed her body to take her back down to lower ground. All her energy had been drained away. She had to give in. Her eyelids heavy, she lay down and closed her eyes.

*****

Lauren jumped as she woke from her vivid dream, a faint light from above the stairs making her squint. Was the door open? Hours must have passed since she'd been cocooned here in this nightmare of squalor. She'd given up shouting for Max long ago, needing to save her energy.

She didn't move – her body wouldn't allow it – but she knew this could be her chance to escape. Somehow, she had to make it up the steps to reach the gap in the door where the light was streaming in. If she tried really, really hard, she thought she could do it. So, with half-open eyes, Lauren stood up. She felt dizzy, her head spinning like she was on a merry-go-round – but without the thrill of excitement.

As she scrabbled across the earth she tried to ignore the raging ache running through her body, and – with the light beckoning her – she ran, taking two steps at a time. One more step and she would be free.

As she took her next stride towards the door, however, it suddenly slammed in her face. She tried to grab the door but she fell to the floor in a heap, utterly exhausted. There was laughing coming from the other side, a laugh she'd recognise anywhere… it didn't happen that much, but when it did she couldn't mistake it. Max had a laugh like a hyena.

Determined not to cry, Lauren stood up and shook herself. What was Max up to? Why was he keeping her locked up here? She didn't understand. "Max," she rasped, 'if you're there, can I have some water?" Her voice was a whisper, her dry throat making her hoarse. "Max, please, I need water!"

Suddenly a noise came from the bottom of the door and a ray of light entered the room. Lauren could just make out the bottles of water being pushed through a hatch. A sandwich on a small tray was also placed on the floor. The light dissipated as the hatch slammed shut.

Trying not to think about what Max was doing – or why there was a hatch in the door – Lauren picked up the bottle of water, using all her strength to open the screw top. She hadn't realised how weak she was. Guzzling half the bottle of water without taking a breath made the liquid escape her mouth and trickle down her chin, and next she grabbed the sandwich, forcing herself to take big continuous bites as she quickly swallowed. Soon she began to heave as her body convulsed into spasms. The liquid and food felt alien to her. Lying down, she let the rest of the water refresh her.

The extreme pain in her abdomen took a while to ease, but when it did she sat up and began feeling along the bottom of the door. Nothing. Where was the hatch? She dragged her hand over the coarse wood, feeling the space of a lock. A rounded hole at the top and a small oblong shape at the bottom brought her a wave of euphoria, and spreading the mound of earth away from the top step, she reached for the hidden keys. Her hand found the set, but inserting the first key into the lock proved tricky; her coordination was lost in the dark. She fumbled around, the key scraping against the metal but not connecting. She tried the second key. With the realisation that neither of the keys fitted, she screamed out, "No!"

Max

After all his preparations, Max had finally built his dungeon-like prison. It was secret, dark, and scary. The basement floor was still full of earth set on concrete floor slabs, and Max was enjoying excavating it. The basement walls were looking dull and dirty, and he was more or less getting used to the lingering odour. The ugly poles dotted around helped make it even more dungeon-like. Every moment he'd spent working down there, he'd felt the eerie atmosphere as it surrounded him, closing in on him. It was perfect.

Max smiled to himself. He'd been rehearsing this moment in his head for months, and now, with Lauren locked in the basement, his plan was finally in action.

Chapter Eighteen

Throughout the last two days, Lauren had learned to navigate her way around the basement. She'd also located a large round utensil, and had used it to build a makeshift pit toilet, far away from the steps; after going to the toilet she'd scoop up handfuls of fresh earth, piling it on top of her urine to hide the stench. Faeces were discarded in the same way, though having hardly any food gave her intestines no reason to contract that often.

The sandwich of cheese and ham and the two bottles of water she received daily gave her something to focus on, but although she'd tried every trick in the book, she couldn't get Max to communicate with her. Talking calmly, shouting, flirting… nothing worked. If she was going to get out of here, she'd have to play a tactical game with him.

Standing by the door, she waited for the hatch to open and for the tray to be hand-delivered to the spot next to her, and although the small bit of light seeping through slightly blinded her for a few moments, she welcomed it. Anything that pushed back the darkness, even if only for a moment, was something to savour.

This time, Lauren decided to try a different approach; as her daily picnic was delivered, she picked up the sandwich from the tray and slung it at the gap in the door. She wasn't sure whether the food had landed on the other side or not until…

"Now, now, Lauren, don't be like that. Don't be so ungrateful!" sniped Max.

"Max, please, can we just talk?" Lauren asked, amazed he'd even said anything after two days of radio silence.

"Talk? What about, my sweet?"

"Tell me why?" she pleaded.

"Tell you why? You'll know when I'm ready to tell you. Do you hear me?"

"What a weak man you are, Max Davies," Lauren said, wanting to goad him into a reply.

"You asked me why, Lauren. Well, you'll find out in time. You have to be patient."

Lauren was exasperated, but felt pleased that she'd finally got Max talking. She needed to keep this going. "You can't keep me here, Max," she said.

"Yes, I can."

"Someone will find me. Chloe will wonder where I am."

"That's been taken care of, Lauren, so there's no need to worry. All your friends know that you're very ill and have taken to your bed. I told them it would likely be two or three weeks before you'd begin to feel better."

"Max, please let me go – I promise I won't tell anyone you kept me here against my will," Lauren pleaded desperately as a tear ran down her cheek.

"You're a joke, Lauren," was his only reply.

A second later Max appeared in the doorway, his stance like a predator waiting to capture his prey.

Lauren froze, sweat pouring down her body even though she remained still, and when Max looked her up and down, she whimpered. She tried not to breathe too loudly but it was impossible; she was shaking as Max's face contorted into a grimace. She felt cold tears streaming down her face, and when she opened her mouth to scream, nothing would come. Her legs felt like jelly; she couldn't move. Closing her eyes tightly, she balled her fists, knowing she might have to fight for her life. A lump grew in her throat and she let out a long sigh.

When Max started walking towards Lauren her legs collapsed beneath her, and moaning loudly, she lay on the cold ground, shaking violently. He was coming for her. This man who she'd once adored was now like a wild animal, tormenting her like she was his next meal.

He moved his position, crouching down to be on her eye level. Then, his nostrils snarling, he grabbed her cheeks with his thumb and forefinger, squeezing tightly. He didn't speak. He held on for several seconds, and then – just when she couldn't take it anymore – he released the tension from her cheeks, turned around, and left. When she heard the turning of the lock she wondered what his game was.

Lauren waited for a few seconds to see if anything else would happen, then she rolled into a ball and started sobbing loudly, digging her nails into her skin. She just couldn't stop shaking or crying. In that moment, she felt nothing. Nothing but hopelessness enveloped her. No one was coming to save her.

*****

Ever since day one Lauren had been keeping track of everything she could see, hear, and do. Even when she was feeling completely helpless and hopeless, she remained as observant as possible, remembering as much as possible in order to predict Max's next move and – hopefully – plan her escape. She'd been placing some small sticks she'd found into a line in the earth, the hairgrips she'd been wearing that fateful night occupying the same area, in case she needed them at some point. There were now four sticks, signalling the four days (as far as she knew) that she'd been shut away in this filthy hellhole. Personal grooming, of course, was impossible; using one of the bottles of water from her daily allowance, she sometimes tried to have a quick wash, but it just wasn't practical. Her hair was matted, and she could no longer run her fingers through it.

Throughout these last four days, she'd learnt many things about her surroundings. She'd been trying to discern patterns and establish routines of when Max came and went, when the hatch was opened, and when food odours seeped through under the door. All these habits had contributed to her awareness of time. She began to recite *A Dream within a Dream* by Edgar Allan Poe, one of her favourite poems. This kept her brain mentally sharp, plus some of the words resonated with her captivity. 'That my days have been a dream; while I weep – while I weep!' *How true that was,* she thought.

The familiar sound of a door being opened made her flinch. She could hear him coming in. There was a long pause as a shaft of light flickered, its beam piercing the darkness and seeking her out, nosing into all the corners. She held her breath. After a few moments, the light switched off. She could hear breathing, his stale odour consuming the room. She stood poised with her legs braced apart, shifting her body weight from the balls of her feet as she brought her own breathing back under control. There was a pleasure in his breath, like an animal on heat. He did not speak. She felt a draught of air as he walked past her, then a scraping sound – like a large object being dragged along the floor – alerted her senses. She heard a click and the room filled with a bright light. Lauren had never felt such pain as the light seared into her vision, blinding her, her eyes watering under the intensity. As she acclimatised to the glare, she knew instantly what the treadmill was for.

Lauren looked at it with dread as Max started pulling it towards her. As he approached, she flinched. This man in front of her was a monster.

His eyes widened as he beckoned her to stand upright. "Undress, Lauren."

Those two words threw her for a moment. "What do you mean?"

"Get the bloody camisole set off, *now*. Look at the state of you, Lauren. You're a mess." Max glowered at her.

"Take it off – why?"

"Just do it."

"No – I refuse."

"You refuse me?" Max stepped towards her, raised his hand, and slapped her hard across the face.

She lifted her hand to her cheek as she fell to the ground. "You bastard!"

Max grabbed her arm and pulled her up, her feet dragging behind her.

"Get it off now! Don't make me repeat myself." Max stood in front of her, waiting and watching.

As she removed the blue camisole set she'd never felt so vulnerable; standing there in her nakedness, she felt weak, ashamed, and embarrassed. When she'd walked into the expensive emporium, the beautiful blue silk camisole set was the first piece of gorgeous bedroom wear she'd noticed. It was costly but she thought it would not only be a present for her but for Max too. As it dropped to the floor it looked more like a dirty dishcloth than any fancy lingerie.

"Do you think for one minute that I actually loved you, Lauren?" Max sneered, his eyes looking her up and down.

She folded her arms across her breasts, trying to hide her modesty.

"Get on the treadmill. Go on, move – now!"

Trying to ignore his hurtful words, Lauren shuffled forwards, taking a step up onto the treadmill and balancing her body on the cold black rubber. Max picked up the blindfold from the chair and tied it tightly around her eyes.

"Max, please."

"Please, what?"

"What are you going to achieve?"

"Wait and see, Lauren, just wait and see."

He moved her towards the front of the treadmill, and a second later Lauren heard a click. The treadmill moved quickly, causing her to fall. She landed face down in the earth.

"That wasn't very good, Lauren, was it?" came Max's condescending voice. "You need to learn how to stay on it."

"I can't do it, Max."

"Yes you can, and you will – even if it takes you all night."

Lauren couldn't fathom out Max's game, but she knew damn sure that she would beat him.

Max steered her back to the front of the treadmill and the cycle repeated. On the fifth attempt, Lauren began to sense the tempo. Her fatigued body was going through persecution but she was going to win.

This time she managed to remain upright and run. Her mind took her back to the days when she was younger and she'd go to the gym straight from work; she'd been an expert on the treadmill back then. She'd learnt how to grab the handrails, and how to place her feet onto the sides of the belt. The belt would start to move at a slow pace, and then, one at a time, she would place her feet onto the belt as she released her hands from the handrails. Conquering the machine in front of Max put a slight spring in her step.

Now that she was doing well, Max quickly became bored with the game, even though he'd been planning this for weeks. Reaching out, he turned the treadmill off and Lauren immediately sank to her knees. She slid off the end, but she sensed a victory.

Even so, she didn't feel well. Her racing, pounding heartbeat made her lightheaded, and the heaviness in her chest made her face flush. Her legs, arms, feet, and hands tingled as blurriness obscured her vision beneath the blindfold. She was so hot, even in her nudity, and as she tried to take several deep breaths to calm down, her vision became darker and narrower, like when you pressed down on your eyelids to see stars. Lauren had loved to do this as a child. She loved to see the bright white movement of specks it produced. She blinked hard to shake the white dots away. It didn't work.

Full of fury, Max tore the blindfold from her eyes, and as her eyes adjusted to the brightness, Lauren knew instantly what the rope beside the chair was for.

Max forced her to sit on the metal chair, nudging her feet back until she felt the cold legs of the chair touch her warm skin. After pushing her arms together, Max grabbed the rope from the ground. Thinking that the appearance of compliance could be her best weapon, Lauren presented her hands to be tied, though she let out a squeal as she felt the rope dig into her flesh. She was sure it had drawn blood. As Max twisted the rope around her ankles she felt the rough fibres tear into her skin. Immobilised in the chair, a groan of agony escaped her mouth.

Lauren could smell the greasy sweat oozing from Max's body. Bile rose in her throat, and just as she started to heave Max slapped a heavy strip of duct tape over her mouth. The sense of asphyxiation made her panic, and she quickly tilted her head from side to side to make the liquid trickle back down her throat. Her eyes darted left to right, but she couldn't see any movement; the brightness she'd only just adjusted to had evaporated, the darkness having come back with a vengeance. Max was gone.

Bound and trapped in this tiny space with no food or water, Lauren was terrified. She felt vulnerable and small, but even so, she was certain of one thing: she would not be beaten. Her eyes scanned the room as she tried to focus, and when her eyelids began to droop she shook herself awake. She didn't want to succumb to sleep. She needed to concoct a plan to escape, put an end to this torture. No longer did she want to be at the mercy of Max. And yet still the same old questions swirled around her head: why did he target her? What motivation did he have? And what terrible, twisted mindset was she up against?

*****

It had been hours since Lauren had been left bound to the chair without light, though she couldn't work out how many exactly. Eventually she heard the known footsteps returning, and in a panic she bolted upright in the chair. Max yanked the duct tape from her mouth, though she couldn't speak even if she'd wanted to. He force-fed her some liquid from a spoon, making Lauren cough and splutter as spoon after spoon was repeatedly inserted into her mouth. The liquid tasted smoky, like whisky. Max held her cheeks, squeezing them together, pushing the liquid down her throat. She could feel the overspill running down her chest and onto her breasts. He continued to force-feed her the liquid, and while she tried to wriggle in the chair, nothing seemed to move. She felt like she was choking. Max stopped when she started coughing profusely, and the next moment she projectile vomited all over him.

"Naughty, naughty girl," said Max as he left her sitting in a mixture of whisky and vomit.

The period of time she'd been choking had left her without oxygen, decreasing the blood flow to her brain and causing her to nearly pass out. Lauren felt like she was locked in place. Sitting so long was crushing the life out of her muscles. In her mind, she revisited the days before she'd met Max and her life was normal. Then oblivion took over.

*****

When she woke, a single mattress lay slumped on the earth. When had Max put it there? She had no clue. She also wasn't tied to the chair anymore. He'd allowed her some light – a camping lantern that emitted a faint orange hue. There was no sheet or blanket on the bed, but there was at least a piece of clothing. She pulled the black oversized shirt over her head, enjoying the feel of the soft fabric against her skin. She felt grateful for such a small mercy. There was a chocolate bar too – she grabbed it before crawling onto the small mattress, the plush surface actually feeling pretty comfortable. Was Max softening her up? Or did he want her to remain strong for something else he'd planned for her? Whatever it was, in that moment Lauren didn't care; she was too focused on the chocolate bar. She unwrapped it, eagerly taking a bite. She could have easily eaten the whole bar right there and then but she knew she should keep it for when she was desperate. A few more bites helped regulate her blood sugar level, giving her back the energy that had evaporated from her body. Although desperation was setting in, she knew she had to fight.

Surely Chloe would soon realise something was wrong. She needed this thought to keep her strong. Her head hurt, and she felt nauseous, tired, and dehydrated. Then it hit her: it was a hangover. Recalling yesterday's events proved difficult – her short-term memory was impaired – but brief flashes of memory shocked her.

After a few minutes Lauren had regained her composure, though her adrenalin was pumping so fast her heart felt like it was going to pound right out of her chest. She'd be much better off if she could control herself, control her body. Her observation and memory had kept grips of what was going on around her right since the beginning of her captivity, and she needed that to continue, though her strategy of taking one day at a time was beginning to nudge her towards negativity.

Her emotional outbursts were worthy of nothing. She didn't want to grovel, beg, or become hysterical, and she certainly didn't want to cry any more in front of Max. She needed to show him that she was worth his respect. His paranoid delusion must have him thinking she was conspiring against him, so she needed to change this as soon as she could. Lauren knew that if Max felt like he was losing control, he might react with more violence.

So, the next time he interacted with her she would be a good listener; being empathetic towards him might make him be more benevolent towards her. A topic like family, for instance, could see him open up to her. She knew he'd had a powerful bond with his mother, though he never wanted to discuss it with Lauren – ever. Perhaps she could use that.

Max

Writing a ransom note takes careful consideration and planning, and Max knew he had to get it right. He had to be clear about his demands. Consequently, he'd spent a lot of time choosing just the right words:

Now listen carefully, Jacob. At this present time I have your sister Lauren in my possession. She is safe for the time being. If you want to see her again you must follow my instructions. You will notice a plane ticket to London attached to this letter. It is for Thursday night. You will be on this flight and you will make your way to this address:

12 The Close,
Heptonstall.

If you value your sister's life you will act straight away. It's in your best interest if you do as I say. No police – or it will be too late to save your precious sister.

From,
Your dear friend,
Max Davies.

Chapter Nineteen

As the plane met the tarmac, Jacob was at a loss as to what his next move should be. Was he to meet Max at the address on the ransom note, or should he involve the police? He didn't want to put Lauren in any more jeopardy than she already was, and he didn't want to add any more danger to her life. Could he do enough to save her from the clutches of Max Davies himself? He certainly hoped so.

Jacob reflected on the last time he'd spoken to Lauren. She'd appeared happy and relaxed, loving her job and her new boyfriend. What wasn't there to be happy about? The new boyfriend, Max Davies, turning out to be a criminal – that's what. It had been such a shock to Jacob, who immediately blamed himself. After all, he had brought Max Davies into her life.

Jacob had traced Max back to an agency, Acorn Recruitment, who often sent teachers to work in Lauren's school. Max had been working under the name Reynolds; Jacob had spoken to Michael Brown, the Managing Director of Acorn Recruitment, who confirmed that a complaint had been made against a Mr Reynolds. The tattoo on Max's neck had blown his cover. He'd been rude and unprofessional and he hadn't reflected the caring, professional role he needed to when working with the children at Salford Primary School. The agency had been told that Salford Primary no longer needed his services.

Jacob knew that the first seventy-two hours were vital when it came to missing persons, and in Lauren's case, it had long since gone past that. He hadn't mentioned Max's ransom note to his mother – he'd been in a dilemma ever since he'd opened it – and the decision to take on Max's threat alone was making him question if it was the right thing to do. As a backup he'd managed to locate Chief Inspector Mann of the Manchester Police, and after a few white lies he was able to get his phone number too – at least he had a contact in case anything backfired. For now, he had no choice but to go solo. His priority was to get his sister back – at any cost.

He checked into a hotel room one mile away from the address. An old lady with greying hair sat behind reception; she looked Jacob up and down before handing him a key displaying the number 28. "Top of the stairs, then turn left," she muttered.

Jacob had chosen the remote hotel, which was circled by emptiness, for that very reason; he didn't want prying eyes, not now he was this close to finding Lauren.

The hotel was minimal, its decor reminding him of an old-fashioned motel he knew on the outskirts of Ontario, Canada. The ornate silver doorknob was the only luxury to his room; inside, it was a whole other story. The seventies theme hit him as he sat down. The red threadbare carpet bearing coffee stains matched the red chair that was placed under the window. A single bed perched in the corner, off-white sheets matching the off-white walls. The toilet and shower had engrained mould etched into the grey grouting. And yet, even with all this going on, somehow the room felt comfortable; the aged characteristics relaxed him.

His first thoughts were how he was going to get his hands on the array of weapons he needed to equip himself with. He would need to drive into town and pick up items without causing suspicion. He'd passed the high street earlier, it wasn't too far away. He looked around his hotel room. Yes, this would be large enough to practice in. He wanted to be fully prepared for Max.

Gathering his wallet and the keys to his rental car, he made his way downstairs. The old lady in reception had remained in the same spot, her head just in view over the front desk. She nodded at Jacob as he walked past. Jacob acknowledged her, giving her a half-smile. In return the old lady beamed back at him.

Jacob entered the hardware store feeling confident and relaxed. He didn't want any unnecessary attention as he shopped for weapons.

A short chubby man with a balding hairline greeted him. "Can I help you, Sir?"

"Just having a browse, thank you," replied Jacob.

He headed straight to the knife section – after all, he would require a knife to defend himself with. They were all displayed in separate boxes in a silver cabinet covered with translucent glass, and after a quick browse he spotted a three-inch lightweight knife made of 3mm-thick stainless steel, sturdy enough to hold up in a fight. It also had a pocket clip, which would make it easier for him to carry. Next was a stun gun. This would be useful, he thought, as they were non-lethal and could immobilise a target for a minimum of five seconds. Jacob then added pepper spray to his consignment: it would be quick and easy to use, and extremely effective, causing severe irritation to the eyes, skin, and respiratory system. He knew it wouldn't stop Max, but it would slow him down.

He continued his walk around the store, soon coming across a Defender torch. What Jacob liked most about the Defender was its two different light output levels – a high-powered beam at five-hundred lumens would be bright enough to temporarily blind Max, allowing Jacob time to get away. He especially liked that you could use it at a distance. The Defender had a Total Internal Reflection lens that allowed maximum visibility, but it also had a five-lumens low beam so he could use it as a normal flashlight too. If he could see what's coming, he'd have a better chance to react and prepare himself. His last item was a personal alarm, which was small and which he could attach to his keys for easy access. At one hundred and thirty decibels, the alarm would grab the attention of anyone close by. It was also equipped with a backup whistle in case the alarm batteries failed. His only hesitation with this kind of self-defence device would be relying on others for help, but perhaps this alarm would scare Max enough to think twice.

The retailer didn't display any astonishment towards Jacob as he scanned the prices of the individual items. He simply packed them securely and handed Jacob the bag.

"Have a good day, Sir," he added, giving Jacob a wink.

"Thank you, I will." Jacob took the bag, leaving the shop with an air of satisfaction. His purchases had been made without an ounce of wariness. This boded well.

Returning to his hotel room, Jacob placed each of his weapons neatly onto the bed. He needed to know everything he could about these pieces. Different safety mechanisms could be tricky to operate and Jacob knew they would slow him down if he didn't know how to operate them properly. Things like switching off a safeguard, pressing the right button, or uncapping pepper spray were all things he needed to practice beforehand. He took each object, inspecting them one by one and becoming as familiar with them as possible, practising with each one until he could use them all efficiently.

Tomorrow would be the day he'd encounter Max Davies, and Jacob was ready for a fight.

*****

It was time. Lauren crawled around on all fours, desperately trying to find an escape route. She scoured the earth meticulously, using large sweeping motions with her hands. She would cover the whole surface area, not missing even an inch. She simply had to get out of that basement – there was nothing else for it.

Suddenly, she felt something different. There seemed to be some sort of seal in the ground. Frantically pushing the earth away and feeling her way around the asymmetrical shape, she pulled hard on the raised piece of board. It was a trap door. While she wondered what lurked beneath, her heart began to beat faster as adrenalin pumped deliciously around her veins.

There was a discarded torch lying on top that she quickly snatched, pressing the button and causing light to engulf the trap door. Still feeling weak but making use of the adrenaline, she pulled the wood back on its hinges. Fortunately, the wood was rotten and it came away far more easily that she'd expected. As soon as the trap door was open, several venomous funnel weaver spiders spilled out, making her scramble away in alarm. She hated spiders. Her heart was pounding in her chest, but though she was frightened, it wasn't enough to make her turn back. She was so close!

Trying to ignore the spiders as they scuttled across the floor, she went back to the trap door, shining the flashlight in front of her. The whiff of a foul odour met her nostrils, but again, she ignored it. The torch didn't pick up much of the hole, but there wasn't anything else for it: easing herself down, she followed some steps down into another small crawl space. It smelt like rotting iron pipes, and using the torch to look around, she saw a faucet and a ventilation grille. She thought it could be a bomb shelter. At the other end of the space there was a ladder, and going over to it, she pointed the flashlight upwards. She couldn't see where it went. Slowly, she put one foot on the bottom rung, apprehensive about ascending to the top. Perhaps she'd do a sweep of the room first, come back to it later if there was no other way out. She took another look around the small space, noticing the strange gooey masses that hung like icicles in every corner. She moved some of this weird goo away from her face as she moved forward but it stuck to her fingers. She wiped it on her t-shirt, shuddering; it was the most repulsive substance she'd ever felt.

Looking around again, she noticed a hole in the back wall of the room. Was there another secret room? No, it was a window! Lauren couldn't believe her luck. It had been here all this time. In her elation she lost her balance and fell to the ground. She took several long, deep breaths, then she pulled herself up, trying to stand. Her arm crippled with pain, she winced as she shuffled over to the window. She could feel pain shooting up and down her body. Her hands were cold and covered in blood.

Even with a worn-out body, this was still the perfect situation to escape; she needed to take full advantage of the opportunity even if her chances didn't seem that great. If she remained here any longer, she was certain Max would kill her. It was the risk of escape versus the risk of staying put. The calm that followed was brought on by the sudden realisation that she could leave, though she still had the advantage of all the adrenalin running through her body. She realised this was her best chance and she was going to take it.

With a half-smile on her lips, she looked at the window beckoning her to freedom.

A noise from behind took her by surprise.

He was here.

Her escape had failed.

Instantly, she felt numb, the adrenaline draining from her body as quickly as it had appeared. Silently, she turned to face him.

"Well, well, well – my little sweet is trying to run away from me," Max said, almost in a whisper. He stood with his feet shoulder-width apart, his body balanced, his body language very much showing Lauren that he was in charge again.

Fear gripped her, goosebumps dancing on her skin.

"Let me go, let me go!" screamed Lauren, as loud as she could.

"Shush, Lauren, be quiet," came his eerily calm reply.

"No, Max – no longer. If you're going to kill me, do it now. Go on, you coward. Do it – now!"

"Stop, Lauren!" Max was shouting now, his calmness gone, his voice louder and heavier than hers. "I can't let you go. If I do, he won't come looking for you."

"Who won't?"

"Your baby brother – Jacob."

"Why, what's he got to do with this?" Lauren asked, her voice trembling.

"This is why, Lauren. Jacob has led you to this. He refused to cooperate. He went straight to the top, leaving me at the bottom. He thought he was better than me. We could've been a great partnership. But no, he decided to reject my offer and get me sacked. You see, Lauren? This is why."

"I don't understand, Max," she whined. She was exhausted, and trying to keep up with Max's words was tiring her out even more.

"I know all the details about your parents," Max continued, "about the house you grew up in, where Jacob is... and you know that Mr Reynolds you complained about at Salford Primary? Well, Lauren, that was me."

Lauren shook her head. "No. Max, you're scaring me."

"Good. You should see what else I've got lined up for you, my sweet." Max lunged at her then, grabbing her hair and dragging her along the ground. He forced her to climb the

136

steps, and once at the top, he pushed her to the floor. As he stepped over her he couldn't control his laughter.

How she hated that hyena laugh! She was now so distraught it was taking all of her energy not to cry. Being back in the basement was not want she'd been expecting. The window that had beckoned her to freedom had been her hope of sanctuary, but now it was her violation.

Max

Max knew emotional torture would break her; she was weak, just like her brother. To exhaust Lauren mentally he'd have to get tougher. Jacob would rue the day he ruined him.

Earlier, Max had stared blankly at Lauren, his victim. He liked to see her humiliated. He sensed her shame; he'd injured her dignity and pride. He loved the achievement of his actions, especially when he dehumanised a woman. His lip had quivered with anticipation as Lauren had looked up at him, begging and pleading with him to let her go. Being enclosed in the small space for long periods of time had made her just about give up. Her sleep-deprived body was simply not willing to conform anymore.

How was she going to cope with the next round?

Chapter Twenty

A pasting table had been placed underneath a set of monkey bars. Lauren noticed her blue camisole set laid out neatly on the table. It looked clean and smooth.

"Go and put it on, Lauren," Max said. He'd been watching her ogle the pieces of silk.

Lauren walked slowly over to the table, her fragile body almost giving in to the exertion it took her to move.

"Move, Lauren!" shouted Max.

Lauren flinched, her eyes squinting shut for a second. She remained motionless.

Walking over to her, Max clung to her shoulders, pushing them forward in an attempt to make her move. It worked; the force of his hands on her body jerked her forward.

"Aren't I nice to you, my sweet?" he asked. "Look, all washed and ironed for you." He picked up the camisole set, scrunching it up into a ball and ramming it into her face. "Smells lovely, doesn't it, Lauren? Not like you. You smell like a dead rat." Max laughed loudly. "Put it on."

Slowly, Lauren removed the oversized black shirt she'd been wearing for days. She'd managed to smuggle one of her hairgrips from the shirt into her hand, and she hid it in her knickers while Max was looking the other way. She could smell the washing powder that lingered on the soft fabric, the clean laundry seeming to invigorate her. It felt smooth against her skin.

"Thank you, Max," Lauren said, deciding to use a different tactic.

"That's better, Lauren. Speak to me nicely and I might not be so hard on you."

The black plastic bucket tied with string hung precariously from the monkey bars. It reminded her of when she was at primary school, when her teacher would ask for someone to collect all the bean bags after the PE lesson. Lauren would always be the first to volunteer to pop the bean bags into the large plastic bucket; it allowed her to gain positive achievement points for being a positive role model. Lauren loved to see how many points she'd collected over the course of a term. It would be written in bold print at the top of her school report.

Since being held prisoner by Max in the basement, Lauren had lost count of the time she'd spent reminiscing about memories from years ago. It somehow kept her sane – if she even *was* sane anymore. She had her doubts.

"Lauren, I think you deserve a severe punishment for attempting to break free from me. How dare you. What do you think, sweet?" He said the words casually, as though they were discussing what to have for dinner or what movie to watch.

"I agree, Max. I deserve to be punished," she replied quietly, noticing the expression on Max's face alter. He seemed peeved. Her tactic might be working.

"Okay, Lauren, you win this time. I will save the next punishment for later. Although you've been naughty by trying to escape, I don't think you're in the right frame of mind to commit the right attitude. I will leave you know, my sweet. You can rest on the mattress in your clean attire and I will be back in twenty-four hours."

Lauren wondered what Max had planned for her. For now, though, her tactic had worked, even if it only meant her next endurance test was delayed. She had twenty-four hours to get herself in the right frame of mind, to get her strength back. She'd need it; she sensed something awful was about to engulf her. So far she had kept Max from any elation concerning the encounters he'd set her. If she could just find the stamina to keep this going, it might make him realise what he was doing was wrong. Although, of course, 'wrong' wasn't exactly the right word for what he was putting her through – it was pure narcissism. Pure evil.

She began to think of Jacob; if Max was so tormented by what Jacob had done, maybe Jacob was the one who needed to save her.

*****

When Max returned he didn't waste any time: he got straight down to business. As he walked towards Lauren, he could sense her fear. She was frozen to the spot, her eyes staring in disbelief, her face a ghastly white.

He yelled at her to get up, and as she stood it was clear her thin frame was close to collapsing. He manoeuvred her into position.

To Lauren, the innocent pasting table looked incredibly threatening, and after lifting her lifeless body onto the table, she just lay there, waiting. Her bones had no more strength, her muscles were out of power. She remained still, wondering how she was possibly going to fight back.

When Max was finished, Lauren's legs were restrained and her hands handcuffed together – she couldn't move. It felt uncomfortable being strapped to the pasting table; her back ached and she hadn't even been here that long. The monkey bars looked sinister, especially with the bucket attached, the fraying string that was holding it now at a slight angle. She eyed the drip of cold water as it fell onto her forehead. Another drip came, then another. Her face lay directly underneath where the droplets were falling.

She tensed as another one fell, the intermittent times of the drips beginning to confuse her. Max had left her with light – was this to see the unexpected drops fall? Soon, each drop began to feel like a thud, a loud thump on her skull. The physical discomfort from her head and body being in the same constant position was agonising, the lactic acid having set in very fast in her shoulders. Her back muscles locked up. She wanted to cry. The handcuffs seemed to have got tighter and tighter, the cold steel beginning to cut off the circulation around her wrists. There was no way to relax her arms or to lie comfortably without causing some type of discomfort to another part of her body. The handcuffs weren't the problem;

her neck and every part of her body felt like it wasn't hers. It felt like she was a trapped animal.

As the drips continued to fall, a feeling of claustrophobia began to sweep through her body. How long had she actually been lying here? At first the noise had been more or less bearable but now the noise in her skull seemed louder. She couldn't hear anything else, just the pounding sound of the drips as they fell on her forehead. She tried to sleep but couldn't. She tried to think but couldn't. In that moment, she was only sure of one thing: Max was using torture to finally break her.

Lauren slowly took a breath in and out, but she found that she could no longer regulate her breathing; the long duration of the continued drips were beginning to make her frantic. She tried to cry out, but nothing happened. Seeing each drip coming, but at different times, was turning her mad. The sensitivity on her forehead had her imagining there was a hole in the centre of her head, the drips filling the hole as she sensed her brain swelling.

Then she went to a beautiful place, a place where the drips were warm on her forehead. They cascaded down her cheeks like she was crying. Her sanity was breaking from the noise – she was imagining all different types of things. Good things, nice things… anything to take her away from the torment and discomfort of the dripping water. This didn't last long, however – as a voice inside her head told her *'you're dying'*, she actually believed it this time. She was going to die. And there was nothing she could do about it.

Or was there? Suddenly she remembered the hairgrip she'd managed to smuggle into her camisole knickers, the thought giving her a surge of energy. It was something to focus on at least, something other than that terrible drip, drip, drip.

She wondered how she was going to retrieve it. Rocking from side to side, she managed to push the grip further away from her bottom. If she could somehow nudge it towards her right hand she might be able to set herself free. The concentration made her forget the dripping on her forehead, although the noise was still there, but soon she could feel her lethargic body starting to give up – she didn't feel like she had even an ounce of energy left.

After resting for a few minutes she decided to make one last effort to retrieve it, and as she flung herself on her side, she felt like a contortionist. With her feet restrained and her body on its side, she finally managed to pick the damn thing up. Once she had it she relaxed for a moment, breathing slowly. The next step was going to be the most difficult. Carefully, she bent the straightened metal and placed the tip into the keyhole of the cuffs. Then, trying to be patient, she slowly started twisting the metal in all directions. She knew she was limited to how long she could keep it going – her wrists were beginning to ache already. It was taking forever.

After pausing for rests she knew she would have to ignore the searing pain writhing down her arms and simply keep going. She just had to block it all out for a few more minutes. Trying to concentrate again, she turned the bent piece of metal in the keyway, hoping it was strong enough to depress the locking pawl and release the teeth of the handcuffs. She made sure the double lock disengaged first, taking a moment to appreciate all those police documentaries she used to watch. Clearly, she'd learnt more from them than she realised. Eventually, the metal lifted the locking device inside and with a click the cuffs were open. For a moment Lauren remained on the table, the dread crippling her, freezing every muscle in her body. Max holding her captive had taken control of her entire being, and she wasn't sure she even dared to move.

But she had to. She couldn't come this far and fail now.

With free hands she untied the ankle restraints, her bruised and swollen skin revealing an open wound. As she raised herself into a sitting position, pain rushed through her body. What was she going to do now? Make another attempt to escape? She didn't know if she could, if her body would allow it.

Then Lauren heard the last sound she wanted to hear in the entire world: the doorknob twisted. He was back.

Slowly, she fixed her eyes on Max, frowning at his appearance. He looked like a different person, one filled with rage and pure fury. Facial hair covered his pale white skin and his hair was sleek with grease, his eyes bulging and bloodshot.

As he came at her, she felt his fingers dig into her skin, his squeezing and shaking making her head start to spin from all the tempestuous jerking. She became disorientated as he pulled her from the table, her legs giving way beneath her. As she felt the force of the strike from the monster hovering over her, she noticed her ribs cramping and her breathing becoming harder. Something felt heavy on her shoulders. Was she dreaming? Had it all been a dream? Please let it be a dream!

Her hand touched his as she tried to release his grip, but he just continued to pull her like a rag doll across the coarse, blackened earth. He never spoke, his intense hatred beaming from his eyes. She didn't fight back; she just let him haul her along. He could do what he wanted. She didn't care anymore. She was giving up.

Another heavy blow and she lost consciousness.

*****

Awoken by the sound of banging, Lauren realised that the darkness had returned. Her outstretched hands felt the enclosed four walls; he'd trapped her again, but this time in a far smaller space. She struggled to breathe as her awareness returned, the grinding sound of some kind of slicing tool and a shrill grating noise making Lauren panic.

He was out there. He was determined to terminate her life from the outside world. And this time he'd won.

Max

As he carried the bucket of hydraulic cement to the small maintenance cupboard, he grinned. He climbed the ladder, careful not to spill any. Then, using a trowel, he packed the cement firmly into the holes, smoothing the surface as quickly as possible before the cement had time to dry. He'd mixed the cement to a thick consistency so it would stay up on a vertical surface.

In twenty-four hours Lauren would never be able to escape: the cement would be set, and there would be no way out.

Chapter Twenty-one

Jacob parked up, his hired car blending into the remote area. His hands trembled as he picked up the ransom note lying on the passenger seat. The address was two streets along. The conversation he'd have with Max played again in his mind: he'd stand firm and not accept any responsibility for Max's downfall from Fairfax Financial. He hadn't played along with Max's plan to defraud the company, so in return, Max had decided to kidnap his sister. It was unbelievable. How did Max think he could get away with this? Who in their right mind would plot such revenge?

As Jacob sat in the small black hatchback, he felt like he was in some action film he'd watched on TV – the good guy going wading in to save the hostage – but this was no fiction film, this was reality. He lowered his head, resting it on the steering wheel until a loud noise made him jolt upright. It took him a minute to realise he'd sounded the car horn. His eyes flickered back and forth, seeing if he'd disturbed the silence around him, and in the distance, he caught sight of a shadow.

Holding his breath, he watched the shadow as it walked slowly towards him, soon merging into the silhouette of a man. Jacob inhaled as he felt a spot of perspiration run down his forehead. Wiping it away with the back of his hand, he kept his eyes locked on the man in front of him. He reached for the pepper spray on his belt clip, holding it tightly.

A second later the man stopped, whistling as he opened a wrought iron gate and walked briskly up the garden path, fishing in his pocket for his keys. He put the key in his front door and was gone.

Jacob relaxed, leaning back in his seat as he exhaled deeply, releasing a gasp of air. If he was this nervous now, how was he ever going to free Lauren from Max's clutches?

In that moment, he came to a decision. He couldn't do this on his own – he needed help.

Withdrawing his phone from his trouser pocket, he looked at the screen before searching for his mother's number. He didn't really want to do this but he knew he had to.

Jacob held the phone up to his ear, knowing it would be the most difficult conversation he would ever have. He'd slowly lost contact with his family since his move to Canada, monthly phone calls home soon turning into quarterly ones. Since then, there was always a feeling of uncomfortableness between them both.

He was praying his mother might have some sort of knowledge of Lauren's whereabouts. After all, they were both so close; they told each other everything. Jacob wished he had the same relationship with his mother as Lauren did. On the third ring he heard her voice.

"Jacob! How are you, darling?"

"Hi Mother, I'm good. Mother, you need to listen to me and write down everything I tell you."

"What do you mean, write everything down? Are you okay?"

"Just listen, please."

"Jacob, you're frightening me. Are you in trouble?"

"I can't explain now, but you need to do as I ask. Have you got a pen and paper?"

"Yes, it's right here. I always keep a pen and paper to hand in case of an emergency, and I suppose this must be one."

"Mother, if you don't hear from me within two hours you must ring this number. Jacob recited the eleven digit number. You must ask for Chief Inspector Mann, and you must tell him he needs to go to 12 The Close, Heptonstall."

"Heptonstall? Isn't that where Lauren lives? Are you in England? What's going on?"

Jacob could sense the worry in his mother's voice. "Mother, please just do it."

"Okay, repeat the number again, Jacob."

Jacob repeated the number in a slow, loud voice, then said, "The time is five minutes past eleven. If I haven't called you by five minutes past one, call him."

"I will, Jacob, I promise. Whatever this is… please take care. I love you."

"Love you too, Mum." When Jacob ended the call he realised it was the first time he could ever remember telling his mother he loved her. He smiled. Then he glanced at the time on his phone – he had two hours to save his sister.

*****

Jacob checked his pockets – his weapons were in place, ready to use if he needed them. And if he did need to use them, he thought he could do it properly; the hours of practice had made him feel more confident.

He started the engine, driving slowly to the next street before parking up next to an end terrace house. Lights illuminated black rubbish bins, a cat meowed as it ran across the path. It felt eerie. Still, it was time. He had to do this – now.

As Jacob climbed out of the car his foot got caught in the seat belt, causing the pepper spray to unclip from his belt and go crashing to the ground. It hit the concrete pavement with so much force that it activated, a small hissing sound sending the colourless mist exploding into the air and up to his face.

Jacob ran around to the back of the car, having avoided rubbing his eyes when he'd felt the mist rise up to him. He searched frantically in the boot of the car for a bottle of water as his eyes watered profusely. Trying to calm himself, he took a deep breath, drawing a low, raspy cough. His skin felt like he'd got severe sunburn. Straining to see through his watery eyes, he finally managed to open the bottle of water, and with one fierce movement he threw the water across his eyes and face. He closed his eyes for a while before daring to open them again, letting his eyes and face recover. He took several deep breaths, the air in his lungs eventually returning to normal.

As he composed himself, Jacob wondered if he was really up to this. Was he mentally strong enough – even physically fit enough – to confront a psychopath? Max had once been a good friend, but now he was the enemy. He also hadn't seen him for a long time – he didn't know what kind of man he was now. What was he going up against?

With great effort he pushed his negative thoughts aside, determined to set his sister free.

Heading back to the front of his car, Jacob wondered if he should pick the pepper spray back up – considering the reaction he'd just suffered – but he knew it was an essential weapon to use against Max. Gingerly, he took possession of the spray, making sure it was clipped securely to his belt. He checked the other weapons. The stun gun lay comfortable in his inner jacket pocket. The Defender lay precisely in the outer pocket of his combat trousers. The personal alarm hung loosely on his car key fob. The knife was clipped to the front pocket of his trousers. Fully equipped, he was ready to go.

As he walked slowly towards the house, breathing deeply, Jacob started gaining a confidence he'd never felt before. This was his chance to put things right: to bring Lauren, his mother, and him back together. To be the family they'd once been – his aching heart yearned to be part of his family again.

A surge of adrenalin ran through his body as he approached the desolate detached house, which was conveniently surrounded by fields of nothingness. He knocked the door repeatedly with unabashed force, and when the door opened Jacob stood still in the half-light, willing himself not to run.

"I was expecting you, but not quite this late," Max said by way of greeting. "You've put your sister through unnecessary torture. Were you trying to catch me unawares?" He stood with his body in a power stance – clearly ready for battle.

"It wasn't that easy to yield to your demands, Max," he replied, trying to keep his voice even.

"Really? I thought you'd come running to save your precious sister."

"Where is Lauren?" Jacob asked, speaking in a loud, clear, concise voice.

"All in good time, mate," Max replied casually.

"Mate? You're no mate of mine. Yes, you were once, Max, but now… what happened to you?"

Jacob could see his words were rattling Max; his nostrils flared and his eyes dilated.

"Come in, Jacob, and I'll tell you."

152

As Jacob stepped in through the door, he knew this was it. He would either return back through the door with his sister or he wouldn't return at all.

Max led the way to the kitchen, pulling out a chair. "Sit."

Jacob sat at the table, his eyes frantically looking around the area, absorbing all the details. The window overlooking the open space, the door that had been left ajar, the wooden knife block containing a set of small black-handled kitchen knives.

"I think a strong drink is in order." Max poured brandy into a glass tumbler, filling it halfway and handing it to Jacob. He also poured himself a large one, taking a gulp.

Jacob sipped at his, aware he needed to remain sober. "Can I see Lauren?" he asked.

Max slammed the glass down onto the kitchen table so hard it shattered into millions of tiny little shards, and when he rubbed his hands together blood spurted out like a mini fountain. "Oh shit." He ran to the kitchen sink, grabbing a bright red tea towel and wrapping it around his palm. "Don't make me cross, Jacob – otherwise it's going to be a very long night."

Jacob glanced at his watch: thirty minutes had already passed. Another ninety minutes and his mother would be ringing Chief Inspector Mann – help would be on its way. If he could just keep Max talking, he might get out of here alive.

Max winced as he tightened the tea towel around his hand. To Jacob, the blood he was losing looked like a surplus amount.

"You might want to get that seen to, Max."

"It's a mere scratch." Max held his hand up to Jacob, signalling it was all okay. "Now, where were we? Ah, yes, Lauren. The lovely, sweet Lauren. You can see her… if you can find her."

Jacob jumped up from the chair, sending it crashing to the floor as he lunged towards Max and placed his hands around his throat. "Where is she? Tell me, Max! Tell me why!"

Max struggled to breathe, his face turning crimson, but he still managed to bring his leg up and knee Jacob forcefully in the groin. Immediately Jacob released his hands from Max's neck, falling to the floor as he doubled over in pain. Max kicked him in the face with his left foot, sending Jacob sprawling across the kitchen floor. His head hit the cold kitchen tiles.

For a second he lay motionless before attempting to stand up, and as he did so a high-pitched noise made them both jump. The sound was deafening. Max spotted the personal alarm on a set of keys in the corner of the room; they'd fallen out of Jacob's pocket when he'd gone sprawling across the floor. Max crouched down and picked them up, quickly turning off the alarm button.

"What the fuck is this?" Max held up the personal alarm, dangling it in front of Jacob. "You came here armed with an alarm?" Max laughed, his hyena cackle filling the room. "You are a joke, Jacob, a bloody joke. Now get back in the chair and stay put. You hear me?"

Jacob slowly stood up and sat back in the chair, inanimate. His head hurt and he could feel the sensation of liquid running down his face. He wiped it with the back of his hand, blood smudging onto his fingers.

"You are going to sit there and listen, Jacob," Max told him. "When we met at Fairfax Financial I thought you were an okay guy. You were good at your job and I thought we'd made a good partnership. We could have made millions of dollars, you know."

"Millions of *illegal* dollars, Max."

"Shut up and listen. Thomas Victor wanted out – just like you. Do you know what happened to him?" Max began to pace up and down. "Do you?" he shouted.

"Thomas Victor?"

"He's dead. It was so easy, arranging to meet him at Butlin's Minehead, where your precious sister was for the weekend. Yes, everything fell into place quite nicely. I couldn't believe it when she'd got lost. I thought it would be so difficult. Who'd have guessed she'd walk straight into the trap!" Max poured more brandy into a tall beaker and gulped it down. Then he topped up Jacob's glass. "Drink it."

"I don't like brandy, you know I don't."

"Drink it." Max picked up the glass and handed it to Jacob.

"No!" shouted Jacob.

Max grabbed Jacob's head, jolting it backwards with his free hand before prising his mouth apart and beginning to tip in the liquid, letting it flow into his mouth. Jacob gasped for air as the liquid burnt his throat. He spat the surplus out.

Max stopped, his laughter circulating the room.

"I need the bathroom, Max," spluttered Jacob.

"Upstairs, first on the right. No silly business or your sister will die."

As Jacob mounted the stairs he felt light-headed and nauseous; he needed water to rid him of the brandy he'd been force-fed, eliminating the effects of the alcohol. He couldn't quite focus. Stumbling, he reached for the door handle to the bathroom, losing balance as he made his way inside. He steadied himself by clutching the wash basin, and then, turning on the cold tap, he splashed his face with cold water before talking large slurps of it from his hands.

If he wanted a quick snoop around while he was upstairs he knew he had to be quick; he only had seconds to spare. So, tiptoeing out of the bathroom, he turned to his left where there was a solid pine door. It was shut. He reached for the handle, opening the door slowly, and what he saw inside made him realise, even more, what he was up against. He quickly shut it before running back into the bathroom and pulling the flush. Max wouldn't know he'd been snooping. Looking at his watch, he saw it was now twelve-sixteen. He needed to get a move on.

He felt confused as he ran down the stairs. What sort of person held such a vendetta against another? And for such a small reason, in the grand scheme of things? They hadn't even called the police on him at Fairfax Financial; he'd just got fired! Jacob was sure Max was a psychopath – he had all the traits of one. Max exuded an air of confidence that drew others to him – even Jacob – and he loathed authority, viewing himself as being above the rules. At Fairfax Financial his manipulation and cunningness drove him to try and get what he wanted. This time, it hadn't worked. He couldn't accept responsibility and own up to the mistakes he'd already made. His absence of guilt and remorse over the imprisonment of Lauren showed he had shallow emotional responses. There were no deep emotions hiding underneath his persona. He couldn't be reasoned with.

Walking into the kitchen, Jacob was shocked to find Max wasn't there. Where was he?

Looking around the hallway, he could see stairs leading down to a door, as well as a small carved hatch. Could this be where Lauren was imprisoned? He followed them down.

The rickety stairs were scuffed with marks and had traces of dry mud in the corners. As he neared the bottom, a stench of urine hit his nostrils. An old wooden tray with a half-eaten sandwich had been left on the bottom step. His brain was in overdrive – this *must* be where Lauren was being held captive. He couldn't believe he'd found it so quickly. Cautiously, he attempted to lift the hatch, but it wouldn't budge.

"Looking for this, Jacob?" Max stood at the top of the stairs, a key dangling in his hand.

For a minute Jacob was immobile. Then, unconsciously, he plucked the Defender from the outer pocket of his trousers, switching it on and causing the high-powered beam to shine straight into Max's eyes. The temporary blindness caused Max to fall to his knees, rolling head over heels down the stairs and banging his head at the bottom. For a moment Jacob thought he'd got knocked out but then Max stirred, struggling to get to his feet. Quickly, Jacob pulled out the knife and held it close to Max's neck, the blade almost touching his skin.

"Get up, Max, and walk to the top of the stairs."

"I can't," Max whimpered.

Jacob yanked Max to his feet, dragging him up the stairs. With the knife still at his neck, he frogmarched Max into the kitchen, then made him sit in the chair at the kitchen table.

"Give me the key." The hairs on Jacob's back bristled, a throng of goosebumps coating his glacial skin. He tried to breathe in and out but little air was entering his lungs. He stared at Max and nothing else, blocking out everything around him except the breath that was raggedly moving out of his mouth at regular intervals. He'd never felt so nervous in his entire life. He had to take control, had to curb his shaking body.

"Why so nervous, Jacob?" Max asked, looking into Jacob's eyes with pure hatred.

"I think you're the nervous one, Max. This time, you're on the back foot."

"Really? You haven't found Lauren yet, and I doubt you will. I'd say you're the one on the back foot."

Jacob wasn't about to rise to Max's bait. He knew what his game was. "I'll ask you one more time – give me the key."

"I haven't got it," Max replied. "I mean, I did, until you shone that fucking neon light in my eyes."

"Get up, Max." He pulled him to his feet.

157

"What are you going to do now, Jacob? You're running out of time."

Jacob looked at his watch: it was twelve thirty-five. He had twenty-five minutes left before the police would show up. Hopefully.

"Upstairs – hurry."

Max did as he was asked, but Jacob knew not to trust him. He stayed close, the knife still in his hand, ready to use it if he had to.

"Open the door," Jacob ordered him.

"What, here? Why?"

"I think you know why, Max."

"So you went for a snoop," Max replied, nodding. "I thought you were a long time going to the toilet."

As Max opened the door, Jacob eyed the key still in the lock.

"Get over there." Jacob pointed to the window with the knife.

Max slowly walked over to the bedroom window.

Inching himself carefully backwards, Jacob lifted his hand up to remove the key from the door before quickly running out and turning the lock on the outside, the colour draining from his face as he started breathing heavily. Then, with a burst of adrenalin he ran down the stairs, soon finding himself back at the top of the stairs that led to the hatch.

He knelt down on the top rickety step, frantically running his hands along as he searched for a key. Nothing. He went onto the next step. Nothing. Two steps left and still no sign of it. His heart was pounding in his chest, causing a sharp pain to shoot down his left side. Taking a breather, he tried to relax a little as his hands moved clumsily around, trying to locate the key that would free Lauren. The last step and there it was – just begging to be picked up. Jacob never realised before what a key could symbolise. This key, however, was a powerful one –

it was the key that had deprived Lauren of her freedom, and it was also the key that was going to grant that freedom.

As he took possession of the key he kissed it with his lips before placing it in the lock, and when he yanked the door handle hard, it opened. He was met by darkness, the stench of faeces and urine making him heave. At least the low beam on the Defender gave him some light.

Tentatively, Jacob placed his weight on the first step. The creak was immediate and loud, and he looked around as if he was going to find somebody there. There was no one. After taking another shaky step down he decided to point the light at the wall – no light switch. He took a deep breath as he reached the final step, and as his trainer made contact with the ground his foot sank into thick black soil. Without any circulation of air, the stagnant aroma made it dungeonesque and claustrophobic.

"Lauren, where are you? Lauren, it's me, Jacob!" he shouted at the top of his voice. Silence. Where was she?

What he saw troubled him even more. What had Max done to her? A dirty sodden decrepit mattress had been abandoned on a sea of earth. An empty water bottle lay by its side. He looked at the treadmill with dread. His eyes quivered at the monkey bars, the black plastic bucket hanging sloppily from the top. Images ran through his head of torture. Max had been torturing his sister. He put his hands to his head and cried. He cried for his baby sister and everything she'd been subjected to.

"L…a…u…r…e…n!" Jacob gave a long, loud, piercing cry.

A click of a door shutting and locking made him jump.

He sprinted up the rickety steps and tried turning the door handle, but it was too late. He shined the flashlight in a smooth left-to-right motion at the door.

"You shouldn't have messed with me, Jacob – not before, not now!" shouted Max through the door.

"Max, end this now or I swear I will kill you!"

"And how will you do that?" Max laughed as Jacob heard the footfalls of him walking away.

Jacob felt even more claustrophobic now in the sour stench, the earth, and the dust as he walked back to the middle of the room. The Defender was getting low on battery, and under the dim light his eyes darted to his watch. It was ten past one – he hoped his mother had made the phone call.

His hand trembling, he started searching in his pocket for his phone, getting more and more panicked when he couldn't find it. He searched again and again, but it wasn't there. It must have fallen out in the kitchen during the scuffle with Max. "Damn!" he muttered under his breath.

He decided to turn the Defender off to save some battery, and after dropping to his knees he sat down on the mattress, holding his head in his hands. How stupid he'd been, thinking Max wouldn't have another key to let himself out of the bedroom.

He thought about that bedroom, about what he'd seen in there. Graphic pictures of torture scenes were pinned up on the wall, and while Jacob hoped Lauren hadn't been forced to endure any of these atrocities, in his gut he knew she had. The thought made him angry. He couldn't just sit here and wait!

He turned the Defender back on – the light seemed a little brighter now – and started searching the ground for any clues Lauren might have dropped. He began to look through the soil. Underneath the steps he came across a switch, and when he flicked it on a bright light dazzled his eyes. He blinked to refocus. What he'd seen before was nothing compared to what he was seeing now.

The basement was cold, metallic, and sterile. Jacob observed the ceiling covered in old pipes, winding in twisted angles. A mess of debris lay scattered in the corner. The floor was covered in earth. It was all just so incredibly eerie.

Fear wasn't going to stop him, though. He spotted a tiny key at the bottom of the steps, and picking it up, he blew the muddy dust away. Turning it over in his hand, he wondered what it was for; he couldn't see anything in the basement that required such a small key. He placed it in his pocket, and then, pacing up and down, Jacob scrutinised the place. An image of Lauren rushed into his mind. Where could she be?

His eyes glanced at his watch again: one thirty-three. Where were the police and Inspector Mann? He hoped the inspector had believed his mother, hoped he was coming at all. Then, out of the corner of his eye, he noticed a small clearing of dirt. His eyebrows shot up and he gasped, instinctively jumping backwards.

After a moment he crouched down to scrape the earth back from what looked like a floorboard. Wildly, he brushed the everlasting mud and earth away until a rough wooden trap door came into view, making him gasp again. On the side, a slotted hinged metal plate was fitted over a metal loop, secured by a small padlock. He removed the key from his pocket – it was worth a try. The penetration of the key in the padlock sprung the lock open, and lifting the lid, he spied a smaller basement area, with several steps leading down. In his excitement he went down them too quickly, and when his feet made contact with the hard cement floor his left foot twisted as he slumped, face down. He winced as the burning pain shot up his leg from his ankle, though the pain eased slightly as he massaged it with his other hand.

He looked around the space. There was a disturbed mound of soft dirt in the centre of the room, suggesting someone had already been here. This gave him a lift, and forgetting the sore ache in his ankle he limped towards a ladder that stood erect against the wall. He was surrounded by wood rot, mould, and bugs, and a nasty odour occupied the air. Slowly, he mounted the ladder, dragging his throbbing ankle and trying not to put too much weight on it. As he moved, a spider's web tugged at his face.

Balancing at the top, he noticed the square piece of wood – it looked like a maintenance cupboard – with fresh cement around its edges. Why would there be fresh cement?

Reaching for his knife, he began scratching at the cement surface. Small particles flew everywhere, the tiny grains of dust stinging his eyes. Rubbing them only made them worse.

Jacob banged on the cupboard door with his fist. "Lauren! Are you in there? Lauren!" he screamed.

Stabbing the cement with the knife again, he began to make headway, the minuscule hole that had appeared in the cement slowly growing. He worked on this repeatedly, chipping away the calcareous substance as the skin on his hands became more and more calloused. By now one side of the wood was almost loose – just a little more and there would be enough space for him to slide his hand in and pull the wood free.

He stopped to take a breather – there was a faint knocking sound. Holding his breath, he listened. Another knock. It was so timid; if he hadn't been listening he would have missed it completely. There it was again, a gentle tap. He hurriedly thrust the knife in and out of the cement, perforating the granules.

"Lauren, it's you, isn't it? I'm here – I'm coming for you, my love. Hold on! Give a tap if you can hear me. Please, Lauren. Let me know you're okay!" he yelled at the top of his voice. A light tap tapered away – but he'd heard it.

He slid his hand under the wood, pulling it with such force that it instantly became free. Then, releasing the wood from his hands, it went crashing to the floor.

There she was: her hair matted, her face ashen, her body bruised, and her skin sunken. But she was there.

"Oh my God, Lauren – I love you," Jacob sobbed, his eyes filling with tears.

"I'm alive," Lauren rasped, tears of that realisation and gratitude streaking her face.

Jacob cradled her head in his arms – he didn't want to let her go. "Can you move, Lauren?" he whispered in her ear. Her small hand torch outlined her fragile body. She looked frail and weak.

"Max barricaded me in here hours ago, Jacob," she replied, her voice still hoarse. "Where is he?"

"It's alright – the police are coming to arrest him." He didn't want to lie but he had to give her hope. Besides, he wanted to believe that too. He wanted to believe it with his whole being.

"Get me down, Jacob – now." Lauren began to sob uncontrollably.

"Come on then, Sis," Jacob replied, trying to sound upbeat and encouraging. "Swing your legs around and I'll place them on the first rung. I'll be right behind you the whole way. We'll take it slow." Jacob was aware of how frail and vulnerable Lauren was, and he was worried that if she fell, she would simply break.

Manoeuvring her body around caused her pain, but Lauren had no choice but to ride through it. Dismounting the ladder to freedom, however, seemed to make her panic.

Arriving at the bottom, she clung onto Jacob, burying her head into his chest. The warmth cocooned her cold, shaking body.

Jacob removed his shirt and wrapped it snugly around her. Her blue silk camisole set was torn and dirty. He didn't ask any questions; he knew he'd have to wait until she was ready.

"How did you know I was here?" she asked.

They were both sat on the ground, huddled together. Jacob decided to be honest and not shield her from the truth. "Max."

Lauren shook when Jacob said his name. He squeezed her shoulder and she nodded at him to continue.

"Max sent me a ransom note."

"I don't understand." Lauren frowned, looking puzzled.

"There will be time to talk later, but for now we must think of a way to get out of here. We can't just sit and wait."

"But how did you manage to get in here? I tried to escape, but... he caught me."

"I found a small key at the bottom of the stairs and it fit the trap door."

Slowly, Lauren nodded her understanding. "That was the key I dropped at the very beginning. The trap door wasn't locked when I found it. I nearly escaped – twice. Once when I found the trap door, and then when I managed to free myself from handcuffs. He locked the trap door yesterday. How long have I been here?"

"Three weeks, I think. I'm sorry, Lauren, this is all my fault."

"No," Lauren said, shaking her head. "Don't speak like that. You didn't know he was a monster."

"No, I didn't. Wait – what was that?"

They both listened. They could hear raised voices – something was going on.

Jacob quickly got to his feet, holding out his hand to Lauren and helping her to stand up. He lifted the ladder, barricading it against the trap door, then he put his finger to his lips, signalling her to be quiet. Taking hold of her shoulders he placed her in the corner, remaining opposite to increase their chances of survival. If he decided to stay and fight, he'd need to really commit to it; a half-hearted attempt at fighting back would only put them in more danger.

Getting hold of his knife, he placed all his other weapons in front of him, staring at them – they were all they had to defend themselves. The pepper spray might just incapacitate Max. If he had no other option but to attack Max with his bare hands, he would aim for the most vulnerable parts of the body – the throat, the eyes, the groin, and the stomach. He began to assess their location to decide if they'd be able to escape to safety.

He noticed the silver wire mesh grille covered with cobwebs in the corner of the room. The wire mesh seemed to be held in place by nails; it looked fairly easy to remove.

After thinking for a moment, Jacob grabbed the ladder back up, placing it solidly against the wall. Then, with the knife, he levered the mesh up and away from the nails. Applying his body weight while holding onto the wire, he jerked it from side to side. It came loose just as he nearly lost his balance on the ladder. His foot began to throb, the pain returning with a vengeance. The space was large enough for a person to crawl through. He wondered where it led to.

"I need to check this out – this might be our chance to escape."

"No!" Lauren sobbed. "You're not leaving me. Max might come back."

"Can you follow behind me? Are you up to it?"

"I'm not giving up now, even if my body is," whispered Lauren.

Jacob held onto Lauren's hand, trying to give her some extra strength.

As they both crawled through the darkness towards whatever lay on the other side, they inhaled the dank smell. It made them reluctant to investigate – but they needed to. With trepidation they carried on, lying on their stomachs and using their elbows for acceleration.

A secret door led them into a strange tunnel. A stairway met another tunnel, leading them to a padlocked steel vault door. Jacob tilted the bottom of the padlock towards him so he could see the keyhole, and using his flashlight to illuminate the area, he hit the side of the lock with force, using the knife. The handle of the knife began to weaken. He applied tension on the shackle by pulling on the body of the lock, hitting it with the handle on the side of the lock's body to open it. Eagerly, he wrenched the padlock away from the door. Then, climbing into the vault, he turned to help Lauren clamber in.

Jacob thought the small dark space would be good enough to hide out in – until they were saved.

Chapter Twenty-two

Inspector Mann received the call from Mrs Nancy Adams at precisely five minutes past one. Recalling the conversation and statement he'd taken from Jacob, he had no doubts that this was a severe alert. He also had no doubt that multiple lives were at risk. After an assessment, he immediately made a call for backup, more officers being sent out to the address.

He met the officers at the scene. They already had the house surrounded, but they'd done nothing else so far; knowing two hostages were captured inside, it would have to be a delicate operation, and arresting Max would have to be a tactical exercise.

A police vehicle blocked the drive to the detached house, armed officers taking control of the public's safety.

A while later, six officers were circling the property. Inspector Mann had taken on the task of negotiator; he wanted Max to surrender peacefully for a positive outcome. He needed all parties to resolve their issues and come out of this sensitive situation alive.

Time was passing, but Inspector Mann wasn't worried – it meant that a resolution was closer at hand. Patience is a virtue, he reminded the other police officers.

While Max was quiet now, he hadn't been earlier, when they'd first arrived. He'd been shouting at them, threatening harm against Lauren and Jacob. Inspector Mann couldn't initiate any officers to storm the building, not while Max was so angry. A cooling off period was what he needed.

He'd give it another ten minutes, then he'd attempt to lure Max out and find the whereabouts of Lauren and Jacob.

Max studied the empty bottle in front of him. Had he really drunk it all? How had things got so out of hand?

The police outside weren't going to go away. Lauren and Jacob were trapped. What did he have left? Nothing.

His mother was to blame. Ever since she left him when he was twelve years old he'd had strong emotions concerning death; when he lost his mother as a child, it coloured everything. It made him the person he'd become, the bereavement rooted in his childhood having left emotional scars that lasted for decades. Although he'd felt loneliness, isolation, and depression back then, nobody had sought help for him – he just had to carry on as usual. But in the here and now he'd got himself into this position, and he wondered how he was possibly going to get out of it. There was only one way.

He reached under the kitchen sink and brought out the petrol can, staring at the bright red canister in his hand. He'd filled it up only yesterday.

As he stood there he felt himself sway as nausea rushed through his body. Leaning against the kitchen sink, he tried to focus, though the sound of the bloody policeman shouting through the loudspeaker made it impossible to think straight at all. He was trying to persuade him to give up. In other circumstances, this guy was probably an okay bloke, but he was putting unnecessary pressure on Max and he couldn't think. He needed to think. He had to put in an appearance otherwise the police would storm the house – and he hadn't finished what he'd started yet. He staggered to the front door, leaving the petrol can down by his side.

"I'm still here!" shouted Max, his voice travelling through the letterbox.

"We need you to put your hands up and come outside, Max," said Inspector Mann.

"Not just yet – I need more time."

"Okay, Max, listen to me. We'll give you another thirty minutes, then it's time to come out."

"And if I don't?"

"I think you will," came the inspector's reply. "You're an intelligent man, Max; you'll do the right thing."

"Maybe." Although Max wasn't in control anymore, he knew he had to give them something to grasp onto.

Picking up the red canister, he made his way to the basement, though he stopped in the kitchen to open another bottle of brandy, downing a third in continuous gulps. He already felt drunk but he chose to swig a bit more. The drop left in the bottle wasn't worth keeping, so he drank that too. After dropping the empty bottle on the floor, he picked up a hammer from the toolbox hidden in the top cupboard – he wanted to break some expensive crap. He smashed the small wall-mounted TV to smithereens. The microwave caved into his aggressive strikes. He went completely berserk, smashing up every appliance and expensive item he could see, all reminders of a life he never wanted to lead.

After a few minutes he stopped his destruction; he needed to check on Jacob in the basement and Lauren holed up in the small cupboard space. As he carried the petrol canister he slopped some of the petrol on the floor, leaving a small trail of wet liquid behind him. The stairs looked more intimidating than they had before but he trundled down them, one at a time. Then, realising that he'd forgotten the key to the basement door, he trundled back up.

As he followed his path of destruction, the chaos he'd just made was everywhere. His feet crunching over the shattered glass, he walked to the bread bin, running his hand along the black granite surface – no key. What had he done with it? "Bugger it!"

Staggering back towards the steps he lost his balance, his leg giving out as he went down on one knee. When he stood up

169

again he felt the faintness overtake him; he fell hard down the remainder of the steps, landing at a difficult angle. When his head smashed into the corner of the hard wooden door he lay there for a moment, unable to move. He knew his face was cut, and his tongue found a chipped tooth. Blood had splattered on his clothes. If he hadn't been drunk he was sure he would've felt the searing pain much more.

The red canister lay empty beside him, the odour of the petrol enveloping him completely. Due to the state he was in he knew it was going to be a slow job collecting another one. Still, he dragged himself tirelessly up each step, each one he mounted causing him to scream out in pain. He needed more alcohol to numb the intense agony he was putting his body through. Finally, at the top, he lay there, just for a few seconds.

That voice again. He'd forgotten about the police outside. It didn't put him off retrieving the other canister from the kitchen, though. While he was there he opened another bottle of brandy and poured himself a long drink.

Distributing the petrol evenly proved to be tricky; as he went into the living room, a little splish-splash of petrol trailed behind him. Max paid particular attention to anything inflammable, then to the things he really wanted to see burst into flames. He wished he hadn't lost the other canister but he reckoned he had enough to do what he wanted to do. He looked out the window from behind the curtain, seeing flashing lights, the fire brigade, an ambulance, and around thirty police officers – some of them armed.

Inspector Mann was speaking on the loudhailer, reminding him that they had no option left but to remove him from the property.

Max chose to ignore him. He didn't have much time. The alcohol had soothed his pain a little, and he was ready to go.

Removing the lighter from his front trouser pocket, he limped to the top of the basement, grinning. He knew there was enough petrol down there to cause an inferno; Jacob would certainly get his just deserts.

Outside, Inspector Mann called the swat team to deploy tear gas to assist with the arrest of Max. He hadn't heard from Max for forty minutes, ten more minutes than he usually allowed in a negotiation situation. He had no choice – the safety of Lauren and Jacob Adams was paramount. He needed to force compliance from Max. It had been long enough and he still didn't know their whereabouts, or even if they were safe.

As he gave the order, a huge fiery eruption of light and sound sprayed dusty debris into the air, making the swat team turn back. The noise from the explosion was deafening as wild orange hues lit up the night sky, the smell of burning embers coagulating in the air. An abundance of fireman snatched wildly at the hose, and it was no longer than sixty seconds before water started spraying fiercely like a fountain on the roaring flames. The frantic pace of activity had police gathered at every exit, hoping Max had freed himself from the inferno.

But there was no sign of him. There was no sign of anyone.

*****

"Jacob, what was that?" screamed Lauren. The loud bang and whooshing noise had made her jump.

"It sounded like an explosion... I think the house must be on fire. It's okay though, Lauren, we're safe down here." He squeezed her hand to give her reassurance.

"How long will we be fine, though?" she asked, unconvinced.

For the moment Jacob knew they were safe underground; they had some time before fire and smoke might start appearing through the fire rated door between the garage and the crawl space. "We're safe, don't worry."

"I'm scared, Jacob... really scared."

"I know. Just trust me, Lauren, I'm not going to let anything else happen to you, I promise. Look at me, Lauren." He placed his hand around her cheeks, turning her head slightly towards him. "I will not let anyone or anything harm you. Never, ever again."

Lauren believed him; she took hold of his hand and kissed the back of his palm. "I just want to get out of here."

"We will, soon. We just need to move to reach what I think will be the garage." He knew fire regulations would require the garage to have a window with a small base opening and a trickle vent – he just hoped the house was up to standards.

He started to shuffle along, Lauren following right behind him. The crawl space was getting steeper and narrower, the soil surface making their hands and knees sore. It seemed a never-ending journey but Jacob didn't want Lauren to know that. He was becoming increasingly worried about how this was going to end.

Just then an overwhelming blast of sound and light engulfed them, overloading their senses for a moment. Everything went still as smoke began to seep slowly through their only ventilation – the small vent was closing down on them.

Huddled together, they kept silent – talking would only use up their remaining air. Jacob could feel Lauren's body trembling against his. Time was running out. He couldn't visualise what was going on beyond the crawl space; he just hoped the rescue services would find them soon. The small confined area was causing him to feel suffocated, and he could sense that Lauren was struggling too.

He grabbed at the seam on the neckline of his shirt, vigorously ripping it until a piece tore away. Then, gently, he placed it across Lauren's mouth, hoping it would shield her from too much smoke inhalation. Lauren nodded. The DIY mask would protect her for a while but she could already feel her lungs tightening, making her gasp for clean air. Her arid mouth ached for liquid to ease the pain surfacing down her windpipe, and her head throbbed uncontrollably from dehydration. Her mind revisited the memory of when Max force-fed her brandy. Her body had been ready to give up back then, but she'd kept on fighting – just like she needed to now.

A tapping sound removed her from the memory; Jacob was using his knife to scrape away the corners of the vent. He moved his head from side to side, indicating it was too tedious and would take too long. A faint light was coming from an even smaller space, and as he squinted his eyes to try to focus, he was sure he could see a tiny grille. There was no way the small space would fit two people, though – he'd have to go alone.

Jacob looked back at his sister, who had her eyes closed. "Lauren, wake up." He was worried the smoke inhalation was causing her to become disoriented or even unconscious. He shook her body lightly. He couldn't wake her.

He had no choice but to leave; his priority was to – somehow – find a way to get out of there. If he could find help it would have to be quick. He didn't know how long Lauren had left to live.

Chapter Twenty-three

Nancy couldn't just sit and wait – the not knowing was tormenting her. Her two children were in danger and she intended to do something about it; the phone call to Inspector Mann had made her realise she needed to be there for them. There was no doubt in her mind that her relocation from the countryside to Manchester to be closer to Lauren had been the right thing to do. She'd agonised about upping sticks for months, but now she was so glad she had. Her children needed her help, and she was about to give it. She wondered what she'd be met with on arrival at the address, then tried not to think too much about it.

The late night bus from Manchester was desolate, and Nancy chose to sit near the window, watching the bright vivid lights in the distance over the city. Fear had chased away her sleep and she was now wide awake. As the bus travelled towards Heptonstall, she thought it looked idyllic, even in the dark. Her daughter had certainly chosen a lovely location to live in.

Suddenly, the bus lurched into standstill traffic.

"Looks like an accident," announced the driver.

"Oh no, I hope no one's hurt," she replied.

Nancy looked at her watch. It was just gone two a.m. – Inspector Mann would be at the house by now. He might have already located Lauren and Jacob, but if that was the case, why hadn't Jacob called her? The bus was poised to start again, the traffic having thinned out. Nancy sat back, waiting for her stop, and a moment later the interior lights came on.

"Your stop, madam!" shouted the driver.

Nancy held onto the rail to steady herself; she hadn't realised she was shaking. Slowly, she stood up, taking small steps along the floor of the bus.

"Thank you, driver," said Nancy as she stepped off.

"Take it steady," replied the driver, giving her a thumbs up.

The dimly lit road took her to the end of a street, and as she walked she could see flashing blue lights flickering in the darkness. Her instinct told her to run – to run and see her babies – but she felt frozen to the spot. Standing alone and wondering what had happened, she rummaged for her phone in her bag. She pressed redial and the call diverted straight to Inspector Mann.

"Mrs Adams, hello."

"Hello, Inspector Mann," Nancy said in a shaky voice, "I'm ringing to see if there's an update on events."

"We're currently in negotiations with Max Davies, Mrs Adams."

"Nancy, please. Any news on Lauren and Jacob, Inspector?"

"Nothing to report as yet, Nancy," said Inspector Mann sympathetically.

"Are they safe?"

"I'm certain it will end well, Nancy. A breakthrough is just about to happen. Mr Davies is about to cooperate."

"Can you let me know as soon as you have any news on my children, Inspector Mann?" she asked, her voice giving way to a slight tremble.

"I will call you immediately, Nancy. I know you must be so worried."

"Thank you, Inspector." Nancy ended the call, a tear escaping her eye.

They hadn't been the words she'd wanted to hear from the Inspector; she wanted clarification that Lauren and Jacob were safe.

Determined to find out what was really going on, she continued walking towards the blue flashing lights. A hive of activity was in her sight, uniformed police standing outside the house, rushing here and there as they tried to decide what to do. Well, *she* knew what she was going to do. If the police couldn't do it – she would.

After glancing nervously around her, Nancy walked round towards the back of the house, looking at the lights that were streaming onto the path by the back door but staying in the shadows. Dark figures were walking aimlessly at the front of the house, the sound of their footsteps getting closer. Instinctively, she hid behind a bush for camouflage.

Silent and still, she made herself as small as possible, trying to stay invisible and avoid detection. Her duty now was to save her children, at whatever cost. A fracas appeared at the front of the house as the officer guarding the back door ran around to the front. This was her chance.

Although, at seventy-five years of age, she wasn't quite so nimble on her feet as she used to be, Nancy managed to jog to the back door and step through before anyone saw her. Remembering not to panic, she forced her heavy breathing to subside, though the smell of petrol was overpowering, making her feel nauseous. Now that she was inside, she wasn't sure what to do next.

She heard a voice. It must be Max. He was swearing. He sounded angry and some of his words were slurred.

Walking towards her potential attacker, she kept her hands open to give the illusion she was non-threatening. This just might make him let his guard down, she thought as she went. Besides, he'd probably be surprised to see an old woman in the house.

"Max Davies!" shouted Nancy, loudly.

Max swung around, unsteady on his feet and with a look of shock on his face. "Who might you be? And what do you think you're doing in my house?"

Nancy froze as she registered the petrol can in his hand. Wet patches were splattered everywhere. Realising what was happening, Nancy asked, "Where are my children?" If there was going to be a fire she needed to know now.

"Do you mean Lauren and Jacob?" Max asked, walking towards her and pausing by the armchair.

"Yes, I'm their mother," Nancy replied, speaking in a soft whisper. She automatically recognised something dark and powerful – something that truly, deeply frightened her – in Max. Detecting hate in his eyes, she took a step back. She had never met Max, and now she knew why Lauren had kept him a secret. How had her beautiful daughter got involved with this lowlife? She'd guessed something was wrong with the relationship, of course, but had chosen to ignore it. She wished now that she hadn't.

"Well, old lady, if you think you're here to save them, think again. No one can save them now," Max told her, waving the can in the air whilst removing a lighter from his pocket.

"No! Please, Max, you don't need to do this. I'm begging you! Look, we can sort this out. If it's money you need, I can help you."

"I don't want your money!" Max spat. "Jacob had his chance to save his sister. All he had to do was listen to me, but he couldn't do it." He sighed, shaking his head. "We could have made a great partnership, him and me against the world. We could've made a killing. Ha! Ha! Killing. Get it?" Max rocked his head back, laughing wildly.

"Where are they, Max?" Nancy asked, making a move towards the door.

"Stop right there!" Max shouted. "If you move an inch, I'm going to ignite the whole place." He held the lighter to the can.

Shaking, Nancy looked around at the house. The whole place was drenched in petrol – nothing inside was likely to survive. As she stood there, motionless, her heartbeat began accelerating with fear.

This was no good. She had to do something.

"Go on then, Max, set the place on fire. If you've really hurt my children like you say then I don't have anything left to live for," she told him, calling his bluff.

Max placed the can and lighter down on the living room floor. "You've got guts, I'll give you that – must be where Lauren gets it from."

"Where is she, Max? Can I see her?" Nancy's tone was softer now.

"You can see her on the other side." Max charged at Nancy then, and with one blow to her head she fell straight to the floor, blood seeping out of a gash on her forehead.

Slowly, she opened her dull, cloudy eyes, her strength and wisdom receding like the tide leaving the shore. She wasn't frightened because her life of seventy-five years was over; she was just heartbroken that she wouldn't get to see her children one more time.

Max felt no remorse as her body lay there, immobile. After all, this would hurt Lauren and Jacob far more than he could ever hurt them. His job here was done.

He dragged Nancy's lifeless body towards the back door, then he pulled the release mechanism on the fire blanket mounted to the kitchen wall. Laying it out, he rolled Nancy's body to the centre and then wrapped both sides into her limp, slim frame. Using both hands, he yanked the blanket to the top of the basement steps, kicking her several times before the blanket rolled off the edge. Her body went rolling backwards, jerking up and down before coming to a stop at the bottom. Max heard a thick, crunching snap of a breaking neck or some other bone, and then all was silent.

178

Inspector Mann knew it could take as little as thirty seconds for a house to be completely consumed by black smoke, then another two minutes until it's so hot that everything combusts. He was aware that a modern house like this one – filled with modern materials – tended to reach flashpoint much faster than older houses, so he didn't think Max had much chance of surviving such a disaster. Unfortunately, neither would Lauren or Jacob.

By now a crowd had gathered, watching anxiously, witnessing the flames sucking in the brickwork as it was overrun by the deadly fire. Whispers came from inquisitive bystanders circling in the acrid air.

The inspector sighed. If only he'd reacted differently to the situation then it might not have ended this way. Staring at the house, he took a deep breath, trying to clear his head. There'd be time for reflection later; his prime concern was the here and now. He needed to locate the whereabouts of all three persons – whether they were dead or alive. Hoping for the latter, he made the decision to enter the building. The firefighters had had the fire distinguished within minutes.

"You can't enter the house, Sir. Not until we've given you the all-clear. It's too dangerous."

Inspector Mann looked at the tall figure in front of him, his bedraggled uniform clinging to his tired body.

"I have work to complete here," he told the man, his tone deliberately blunt. "There are three people missing and I have a duty to find them. I will do so at my own risk."

"My men are in there searching, Sir. Wait here a minute."

When the fireman was called away Inspector Mann seized his chance, walking over and entering the building with trepidation. It was a scene of carnage: soot, ash, charring, smoke, and an odour he couldn't quite pinpoint. Nothing had escaped the fire – blackened wood and twisted metal lay all around. There was residue from the extinguishers used by the fire crew everywhere. He heard voices, and as he walked towards them he wondered what they'd found.

"Wait there, Sir, please," said the firefighter as the inspector walked over.

"Is it Max Davies?

"No, Sir."

"No? One of the others, then?" Inspector Mann asked, his heart sinking.

"The fatality is a woman."

"No, not Lauren Adams." Inspector Mann ran his hands through his hair, despair contorting his features.

"We haven't identified the victim, Sir, but we do know the victim is around seventy years of age."

The inspector sighed. Unless there'd already been someone else in the house, the only person Inspector Mann thought it could be was Nancy Adams. But why?

*****

Max took a long gulp from yet another brandy bottle. He'd taken the bottle upstairs to the bedroom, and was now sitting on the bed. The pictures mounted on the wall brought a smile to his face. Pictures of Lauren and Jacob, pictures of torture scenes, even pictures of his own mother.

Climbing off the bed, he snatched at the picture of his mother and ripped it off the wall. He stared at the black and white photograph for several seconds, the face staring back at him hard and lined. Her hair was tied back into a high ponytail, her sunken cheekbones outlining how thin she was. No happy smile to say she loved life. No hint at anything happy at all. She was standing next to a twin tub with large wooden tongs in her hand. It must've been a Monday, thought Max; Mondays used to be washing day back then. He remembered how the whole kitchen would fill with steam, as first the whites were washed and then the coloured clothes as the water cooled.

She was the one who had given him a personality disorder. She was one of those women who had never been a mother to him. Max remembered when he would scream at the top of his voice and accuse her of not caring. She only cared about his twin brother, Billy. Billy had learning disabilities. She loved him. He could do no wrong in her eyes. While his mother always used to mock Max and sneer at him, she would hug and kiss Billy and give him anything he wanted. Max took the rejection hard, feeling toxic shame at not being important or valued enough by her. Her forever changing moods caused him the most pain.

As Max took another gulp of brandy, all those feelings from so many years ago came flooding back to him and he tore the picture into small pieces, letting them scatter to the floor.

He finished the last of the brandy, his mind taking him to places he hadn't revisited for such a long time. When he was a young boy he'd had to learn coping strategies in order to simply get through every day. Having a mother who hated you and gave you no self-worth had isolated him as a child, and it wasn't like he could rely on his father either; he'd never met him. He would've loved to have had someone to play football with, and do boy's stuff with (something Billy never did), but he wasn't allowed to ask about or even talk about his father – it had been forbidden. Max hated his mother for that.

The day he set fire to their house was a day of emotional release. As a twelve-year-old boy he was determined to end his nightmare childhood, and determined to end his mother – after all, she'd never been a proper mother to him. He could remember every detail he'd planned for her that day. He could remember it as if it were yesterday.

She'd gone for morning coffee at Mrs Rafferty's, who lived at number five in their street. It was one of her traditions that he'd remembered ever since he was a small boy. At nine fifty-five, his mother would slam the front door and he would be left to look after Billy. For the next hour he'd have to entertain his brother, but most times he just locked him in his bedroom, pretending it was a game. He enjoyed this time – he loved the silence of the house and exploring things he wasn't really allowed to.

That morning, he'd been thinking about the best way to start a fire. He'd always had an attraction to glowing, flickering, orange flames.

When his mother returned from Mrs Rafferty's, she decided to change washing day, meaning that the paraffin heater would be lit later on in order to dry all the washing. All Max had to do was accidentally overturn the paraffin heater and it would soon ignite all the clothes on the wooden clothes horse. Nobody would suspect anything untoward. He'd make sure Billy was safe, though. After all, he hadn't done anything wrong.

As he'd pushed the heater over he'd stared, long and hard, at the circular wick. Orange and yellow flames began dancing like they were alive as the heat seared and burnt up the wooden legs of the clothes horse. The clothes were quickly devoured by the raging flames as smoke billowed around him, irritating his eyes and nearly blinding him. He needed to inhale, to make it seem realistic. As he did so smoke began to inflame his lungs, and – feeling nauseated – he gasped for fresh air, but it didn't come. He had to grab Billy.

So, Max shuffled along, his feet feeling heavy beneath him as he went. He started panting then, his body soon giving way to long, arduous coughing. He'd done enough. As he gathered his strength he rushed towards the stairs, and with his hands out in front of him he prowled like a predator up each step until he reached Billy's room. Flinging the door open he looked at his twin, lying there with his arms and legs spread out in the cot bed. The rail was up, leaving Billy no escape.

Max grabbed his night light, the torch he couldn't go to sleep without. Then, nudging Billy in the ribs, he waited while his brother stirred. It was another game he had to pretend to play.

Half asleep, Billy was exuberant to see his brother and excited to play this special game. Max told Billy to keep his eyes closed, and not to open them until he said he could. Billy – who trusted his brother completely – traipsed behind Max as he held onto his hand.

Max needed to be quick – the flames were soaring. He dragged Billy down the stairs and out the front door, and then, knocking frenziedly on Mrs Rafferty's door, he raised the alarm.

Max remembered the thick beams of wood, all charred and ash-like from where the flames had licked at them. He remembered his lungs being invaded by the black dust. And he remembered the remains left of a house that had been so alive when he'd been a young boy.

The fire services told him there was nothing he could've done to save his mother. It was a tragic accident, they said; the paraffin heater had never been maintained. Yes, a tragic accident, one that would stay with him all his life.

Max had never once regretted his actions – he'd seen it as an opportunity to improve his life. He went to live with his Aunty Doris, and he never looked back. She'd been a loving, caring stepmother to him, nothing at all like his real mother. His childhood had been bittersweet, but his adolescent years more than made up for it. Eventually, Billy was sent to an institution where, for the first time in his life, his needs were looked after.

All Max wanted to do now was lay down and never wake up. He was tired of living his confused life, he was tired of it all.

He shivered as a wave of emotion ran through him. The bedside lamp looked like a good object to throw, so, picking it up by the brass base, he slammed it onto the solid pine bedside table. Flying debris from the glass bulb covered the cotton sheets, and as speckles of blood dripped down onto the pillow, he realised his head was throbbing – throbbing worse than ever before. He didn't feel in control. He wanted to sleep, but he knew he couldn't. Instead, he dragged his lethargic body off the bed and tried to stand up, though it took so much effort he nearly lost his balance. Slowly, he stumbled to the bedroom mirror, his florid face and red-rimmed eyes staring sadly back at him. His hands were trembling and he felt drowsy.

Making his way to the top of the stairs, he trundled down each step before falling flat on his face. Then, crawling to the dining room on his hands and knees, he reached – yet again – for the lighter. Twirling it in his shaking hand he flicked the flint with his thumb, the flammable fluid igniting instantly to produce a flame. He threw it at the petrol can, and for one second he smiled as the flames roared in front of him.

Chapter Twenty-four

"We've found another fatality."

Inspector Mann stood rooted to the spot, looking downwards. "Who?" he whispered.

"It must be the suspect, Max Davies."

A slight wave of relief ran through him. "We need to search the whole area for Lauren and Jacob Adams. Let's pray they're still alive, though at this point it doesn't look very good," he admitted.

When the police officers and firefighters were given the go-ahead to search the remains of the property, several rushed forward, ready to help. Forensics had already got underway. The fire had been extinguished for more than an hour and they were sifting through the rubble, combing every inch of debris.

Even after many hours of determined searching, Inspector Mann wasn't thinking about his fatigue or the difficulty of the task; his mind was on the two named persons he needed to locate.

*****

"Help!" screamed Jacob. "Is anyone there?"

The air was slowly evaporating, and he was worried about Lauren, having left her in an unconscious state. He believed he'd made the right decision to leave her, though, in order to seek help – there wasn't anything else he could do. Time was running out for the both of them.

He knocked frantically on the grille, but no one was coming to his aid. Should he turn back?

"Are you there?"

They were the words Jacob had been longing to hear. "Over here!" he shouted back, rattling the grille.

"Coming, mate. What's your name?" the fire officer asked, peeping through the wire mesh.

"Jacob. I need to get out of here – I can't breathe."

"Hang on in there, mate."

"Please hurry," gasped Jacob as a shortness of breath caught him.

He started taking deep, forced breaths, fearing that if he didn't, he'd stop breathing altogether. The anxiety and the claustrophobia that had now set in began to increase his heart rate and tighten his muscles. Trying to stay calm, he kept forcing breaths from his lungs, though the desperate rhythm of his shallow breathing was harsh and uneven as he fought for more oxygen.

The fire officer rushed to get members from the rescue team – the team from London and South Central had arrived earlier – and armed with resuscitation equipment and rescue equipment, they entered the garage. The six hundred square-foot detached garage had sustained heavy damage, but it was still erect.

Two members of the rescue team – dressed in burnt orange uniforms and white hard hats –stomped into the garage, grateful to put down the apparatus they'd carried in. They turned to the fire officer, eyebrows raised in a silent question.

"Over here!" The fire officer pointed the way.

The two men dashed to the grille. They knew they had to be quick; they could hear Jacob struggling to breathe behind it. As they heaved the grille away from its hinges with a crowbar, they sensed Jacob was in a dangerous condition due to his lack of oxygen. Slowly, they pulled him out of the crawl space and lifted him onto a stretcher.

Kevin Williams, the more experienced of the two men, applied the oxygen mask over Jacob's nose and mouth, immediately transferring oxygen gas from the storage tank. Kevin then attached a monitoring device to Jacob's finger to measure his oxygenation level. Fortunately, it wasn't as bad as he first thought: his oxygen level was now ninety-one per cent.

Jacob stirred, lifting his hand to the mask to remove it. His agitated state worried Kevin, but he knew he had to remove the mask – he didn't want Jacob fighting against it.

"My sister is trapped in there," he rasped, raising his finger to point at the crawl space. "I think she's unconscious. She needs help – now." He tried to stand up but couldn't manage it.

Kevin placed a foil blanket around him. "We need to take things slow, Jacob. There's a series of questions we need to ask you first, for your sister's safety and for ours."

"We haven't got time for that – *please,* we need to save her!" he exclaimed, a tear escaping his eye.

Kevin patted him on the back. "Okay. Now, you say she's unconscious. Are you sure about that, Jacob?"

"She wasn't awake and she didn't respond to me when I spoke to her."

"Right, Jacob. My colleague here, Eddie Winscombe, is going to ask you some questions. Is that okay, Jacob?" Kevin nodded to Eddie, who came over to the stretcher.

Kevin knew he was going to be the one to make the rescue attempt. At only five-foot-nine, he was of small build, and sufficiently fit and capable of using any piece of equipment provided for the rescue. He was the obvious choice.

It was going to be a difficult procedure, as there wouldn't be enough time to carry out an assessment; testing the air to check it was free from both toxic and flammable vapours would only waste time. Thanks to the small space, there was a potential risk of serious injury or death from the hazardous substances and dangerous conditions, such as a lack of oxygen – Jacob had already shown him oxygen would be a problem. Kevin was well aware that sometimes in a confined space there's a reaction between some soils and the oxygen in the atmosphere – this was most likely to be one of them, though Kevin hoped not. If it was, Lauren didn't have much hope of surviving.

Chapter Twenty-five

Chloe had raced to the house as fast as she could, the commotion in the area making her tense. Her sixth sense had been right all along. How could she have been so gullible, believing Max's lies? She'd known Lauren for years and never before had she had no contact with her for over one week, let alone three. Even when she hadn't seen Lauren for months, she still received texts from her. She should have known.

When she got there, a policeman dressed in riot gear was guarding the scene. "Sorry, madam," he said, "you'll need to vacate this area."

"I'm waiting on news of my friend, Lauren Adams."

"I can't tell you anything at this time. You'll have to leave, sorry." With a sympathetic smile the policeman held out his arm, pointing away from the house.

Chloe turned, giving the impression she was leaving, but as soon as the man looked away, she darted in the other direction. Fooling a policeman was not in her repertoire, but she seemed to have managed it.

Hiding outside the garage, concern grew over her face as she listened to voices talking. From what she could make out, Lauren was being rescued in a controlled attempt by the Manchester rescue team. It was a one-to-one rescue attempt. Immediately she ran into the garage, wrapping her arms around Jacob.

"What's happening? Where's Lauren?" she shouted.

"She's trapped in the crawl space," Jacob replied, nodding to the other side of the garage. "A member of the rescue team has gone in to save her. It's taking a long time."

Chloe closed her eyes briefly, trying to stop the tears from falling. "Jacob, I'm so sorry. I should've realised there was something wrong. I just thought we were losing contact because of Max." She stood back, studying Jacob's face. "How are you? You look like you've been through the mill too."

"Don't worry about me – all I can think about is Lauren. You know, she's all I have left. Mother was killed." As he said the last word, his body threw out a loud, ugly sob.

"Oh, Jacob." She drew his body towards hers, hugging him as tightly as she could. "Lauren doesn't know?"

"No, not yet. I don't want her to know – she's just too fragile. I'm willing her to pull through."

"She will," Chloe told him, "she's made of strong stuff."

"I hope you're right."

Chloe couldn't think of anything she could say to console him. She, too, was extremely scared for her friend.

Chapter Twenty-six

"Lauren?" Kevin asked as he stared at her deathly pale face, her closed eyes, "Lauren? No... don't do this to me... Lauren!"

There was no response to his shouts whatsoever – no flicker of the eyelid, no twitch of the leg. Nothing.

"Lauren!" Kevin shouted again, much louder, and this time Lauren did move – she flinched, opening her eyes so sluggishly she looked like she was moving in slow motion.

"Lauren," he said again, "you had me worried then."

"Huh?" she asked blearily. "Where am I?" She looked around her, her eyes widening when she realised where she was. "No... no, no, no!" she started yelling, tears running down her cheeks again. "No, I can't do this!"

"Yes, you can," Kevin told her. "You haven't gone through all this – come all this way – to give up now, have you?"

"But I can't *physically* do this," Lauren sobbed, shaking her head. "You don't know what I've been through... you have no idea... you just can't know..."

Kevin cleared his throat, talking quietly and calmly as he said, "You're right; I don't know. I've never been through what you've just been through, and you know what?"

She stared at him, shaking her head. She looked utterly powerless, ready to give up all over again.

"I never would have made it this far," Kevin continued. "You, Lauren, are the strongest, most resilient, most amazing woman – you must be to have got to this point." He smiled. "Hey, I'm a wuss – I'd have given up hours ago. Days ago. But you... you're different. You keep fighting until there's nothing left to fight for, and guess what? There's a whole lot left to fight for. You deserve to live your life. Are you going to let one pathetic, unhinged man take all that away from you?"

At the mention of the 'man' something snapped inside Lauren; it was like a switch had just been flicked on in her brain, her soul, her heart. "That bastard," she growled, closing her eyes briefly and taking a deep breath. "He's taken so much from me."

"But no more?" Kevin asked hopefully.

Lauren set her gaze on the man who'd come to help her, a new determination in her eyes. "No more."

Kevin grinned. "Great. Right, let's start again. Put the oxygen mask back to your mouth and re-tie the wristlet back onto your ankle."

Lauren did what Kevin asked. Even though he was a virtual stranger, she felt like she had a bond with this man. His words had moved her, moved her to fight when she thought she didn't have any fight left in her. She was so glad he was here.

When she heard his voice shout, "one, two, three – shift!" she quickly manoeuvred her body. This time it felt like she'd been launched further; she was sure Kevin had tugged harder on the wristlet. They carried on in unison until she felt the wristlet slacken.

"Lauren, I see light – we're at the end!" yelled Kevin, before adding, "Can you hear me, lovely?"

The hope that this nightmare might be coming to an end brought forth within her a sudden burst of panic, but she wasn't going to freak out – not this time. Not now there was actual light streaming in through the crawl space. They were so close!

She snatched the oxygen mask from her mouth. It hadn't been working properly for at least the last ten movements. She'd been counting. Kevin hadn't mentioned it, not to panic her, she supposed. "I can see light, Kevin. Yes, we did it!" Her hoarse voice couldn't mask her excitement.

"You did it, Lauren. *You* did it."

"I couldn't have done it without you."

"I was just doing my job," he replied, and she could hear the smile in his voice. "Now, there are a few things we need to do before you can get to the outside world. Your eyes have been in darkness for a long while so you'll need to wear a kind of eye mask; if you begin to blink quickly it will produce tears that will refresh and rehydrate your eyes. The intensity of light entering your eyes will be consistent and painful at first – we need to protect them."

She hung onto his every word. She had to follow the correct procedures. Her emotions, the shock, numbness, anxiety, guilt, depression, anger, her sense of helplessness... they all needed to be addressed when she was freed. Freed – she couldn't wait. Erratically blinking her eyes, the tears started to flow – she knew they would be the first of many.

"Lauren, I'm going to let go of the wristlet and leave you for just a moment," Kevin told her. "I need to be pulled out by other members of the rescue team. But I'll still be here; I'll talk you all the way through it so you won't feel alone. The paramedics are on standby; they'll be with you straight away. There's no need to worry. Okay, Lauren?"

"Yes."

Up until now, Kevin had insulated himself from the emotion of the rescue; however, his mental mechanism had now been broken. He wasn't accustomed to this feeling. He didn't want to leave Lauren alone, but he knew he had no choice. His immediate physical response to her had grown and he could feel it in his mind, body, and heart. Participating in the stressful rescue together had built a bond between them – one that couldn't be broken.

"I'm leaving you now, Lauren. See you on the other side."

"Don't leave me for too long, Kevin."

"Never, beautiful." Kevin screwed up his face, annoyed with himself. One of his top priorities was to never get involved emotionally with anyone he rescued. He tugged hard on the rope. "Eddie, ready to go!" he shouted as he shuffled along to the opening of the vent.

Eddie was ready for him; he grabbed his shoulders as other members of the rescue team formed an avenue.

As Kevin was hauled out, he wasted no time; springing to his feet, he pulled on the wristlet. "You need to be quick!" he shouted to the paramedics. "She's scared. Get a stretcher!" He turned back. "Lauren!" he yelled. "Ready? One, two, three – shift!"

Lauren responded by using all her strength to push her bottom to the floor, which propelled her body forward – along with the help of her hands. At the same time, Kevin pulled hard on the wristlet, and she hurtled along the ground.

"I can see you, Lauren. Two more pulls and you'll be out!"

She couldn't reply; she was too ecstatic.

"Lauren, did you hear me?" Kevin yelled.

"Yes, I hear you!" she screamed at the top of her voice.

"Let's go for it, girl."

*****

Paramedics continued to check Jacob over. He really needed to be whisked off to hospital but he refused – he wanted to wait for Lauren.

Standing up, he walked over to the crawl space, wanting to be the first person Lauren saw when she came out. When she became visible, Jacob choked back the tears.

As Lauren was pulled out cheers erupted from Kevin's workmates, who stood in a circle applauding him. Eddie patted him on the back. "Well done, mate. Great result."

"It was a team effort," Kevin replied, shaking his head.

"Don't be so modest; you're the hero of the day."

"I think Lauren is." He looked over at her; she was finally receiving the medical attention she so desperately needed.

*****

For the time being, the garage was Lauren's haven. She was safe here – thanks to Kevin. She looked over at her saviour, who was still being congratulated, and smiled. If it wasn't for him she knew she wouldn't have made it.

Leaving his fellow rescue teammates, Kevin headed towards Lauren, crouching down to be on her eye level. Gently, he touched her arm.

"Thank you," said Lauren.

"Don't mention it; it is my job after all," smiled Kevin.

"I think you went above and beyond what you were supposed to."

Kevin shrugged. "As I said, it's my job."

"They're transporting me to the hospital now, to have a full check-up."

"You're going to be fine, Lauren – you're one tough cookie." Kevin winked as he rose to his feet, starting to walk away.

"Kevin." He turned back to face her. "Thanks." She wanted to say so much more, but she didn't know how. He nodded, and she watched him walk away.

As relief flooded through her body, she let herself close her eyes.

Chapter Twenty-seven

When Lauren woke up after the rescue attempt and found Jacob cradling her in his arms, the overwhelming relief took over her whole body; she just felt so happy to be alive. Chloe was there too, holding her hand.

She never thought she would ever get this far, but having her brother and best friend here to support her gave her something to cherish. She squeezed Chloe's hand, though only gently; she still felt so weak. She was pale, bruised, and emotionally scarred. After receiving the heart-breaking news of her mother she'd needed sedating, and blaming herself, she'd become a complete emotional wreck. The thought of her mother attempting to save her only made the hatred she had for Max come flooding back. How was she ever going to recover? The support she'd be cocooned in would help her mend physically, but mentally... how would she heal from the anguish and torment she'd endured? Was it even possible to heal from something like that?

Jacob and Chloe didn't stay with her too long, both of them aware she needed to rest.

*****

Alone, Lauren lay in the hospital bed while watching the national news on TV, every now and again her thoughts leading to her beloved mum. It was her third night occupying the small room she'd been transferred to, and things weren't getting any easier. Blue blackout curtains masked any light trying to come in from the double hung window, and only a dim light emitted from her bedside lamp. Lauren liked it that way. Since her release to freedom she'd uncovered so much –

197

her mother attempting to rescue her, Max dying in the fire.... She hated thinking of Max. She was just numb.

Lauren looked up at the TV screen, listening to Inspector Mann as he spoke at the live press conference.

"The rescue of Lauren Adams and her brother, Jacob Adams, was possible due to a multi-agency approach. We had Manchester Fire and Rescue Services deployed, as well as the Area Response Team from the Manchester Ambulance Service, and we were also greatly assisted by the Technical Rescue Team, who was involved throughout most of the operation. I would like to pay tribute to the cooperative efforts of all the crews involved in this rescue, and I'm pleased to say the operation was successful, despite the conditions at the scene. In particular I would like to thank Kevin Williams for his professional approach and for helping to make the outcome a good one. Lauren Adams is recovering well in hospital and will be released soon."

A tap on the door turned her away from the TV, and after another gentle tap, Lauren wondered why the nurse hadn't entered like she usually did at this time.

"Come in," whispered Lauren.

As she looked towards the door, she saw a shadow lurking outside, and after a moment she realised she could hear heavy breathing – she'd recognise that heavy, ragged breathing anywhere. Her body began to shake. No, it couldn't be. It couldn't be!

The shadow grew and grew, and then – there he was. The tall figure stood in the doorway, making her freeze. Blinking her eyes, Lauren tried to wake up, but she was awake. This was no dream.

Her heart started thumping – she could hear the blood passing through her ears – and her chest started contracting up and down. Her breaths were sharp and shallow. She tried to scream out but no sound escaped. She scrambled to locate the emergency button on the control pad, though she was shaking so much she lacked any mobility in her hands. They remained rigid, unable to grip anything.

"Stop, Lauren. Don't be a silly girl, my sweet."

That voice confirmed her greatest fear.

Her hands came back to life and she frantically pressed the emergency button, feeling a tightness forming in her chest. Breathing heavily, she blurted out, "You died in the fire!"

"Not me, my sweet, though someone very like me. And it's no good pressing that button – I sorted that out before I came in."

Standing tall, Max walked towards Lauren as she cowered in the hospital bed, her face ashen as the blood pounded in the back of her head. Everything was closing in on her again – just like before. She could feel her breath beginning to shake, and then grow rapid. She could feel the trembling of her entire body. Her vision swimming. It was too much. She began to chew on her nails, desperately ignoring the pain as she bit down on the cuticles. Her eyes darted to the door.

"Nobody's coming, Lauren."

"The nurse is due in soon, to give me my meds." Unable to speak normally or smoothly because of her heightened fear, her voice was raspy.

Max stooped over her until she could feel his breath on her face as he exhaled – the horribly familiar odour she hadn't been able to forget. His constricted pupils made his eyes narrow. "She won't be interrupting us, my sweet." His index finger stroked the skin under her chin, making her flinch. "What's wrong, Lauren? A little nervous, are we?"

"You make me sick, you bastard!" Lauren cleared her throat, letting the saliva smear over Max's cheek.

He laughed his hyena laugh. Then, wiping the back of his hand over his cheek, he walked away. Lauren's relief was short-lived, however, when he dragged the chair over to her bed and sat down next to her.

"Oh Lauren, don't you want to hear how I was able to set up my own death, just so I could get my hands on you again?"

"You killed my mother!" she screamed. "You're sick in the head, you monster!" Hot torrents of grief ran down Lauren's face as her body wracked with an onslaught of severe sobbing. A tightening of her throat and a short intake of breath made her feel like vomiting.

"Ah yes, your darling mother – she put up a brave fight. She came to save you, she loved you very much. Do you know what her last words were, Lauren? What was it... oh yes, something like, 'If you've hurt my children then I have nothing to live for'."

Lauren turned her head quickly as she retched, the hot, tangy liquid spewing from her mouth and landing on the floor.

"I had to kill her, sweet. I couldn't let her get in the way. She was feisty, just like you."

Jumping up from the bed like an eagle hunting for prey, Lauren leapt on Max, punching his chest with her clenched fists. Max immediately grabbed hold of her arms, flinging her back down onto the bed. Calmly, he took the syringe from his pocket and stabbed it into her thigh. She succumbed to the lethargy straight away: her legs felt heavy and she became disorientated.

The Propofol would last at least fifteen minutes, Max estimated as he stared at Lauren, his face turning to anger.

He would torment her for the rest of her life. This was just the beginning. By the time he was through with her, she'd end up so damaged she wouldn't have even the resemblance of a life.

When he'd found out she'd survived, he'd had to quickly think of a backup plan. He'd never be able to capture her again, but he'd sure as hell make her life a misery.

A satisfied smirk on his face, Max stood and watched her as she slept.

Lauren woke to find the room out of focus. It was as if a filter were covering her eyes. Her partial unconsciousness had left her weary and she couldn't remember what had happened to bring her to this state.

As her eyesight slowly regained focus, she noticed a blurry figure sitting in a chair next to her bed. She blinked intermittently, and when it dawned on her who it was, she started shaking with terror. The monster who tortured her was here, ready to repeat her nightmare all over again. How could that possibly be? She drew her legs up to her chin, wrapping her arms around her knees as if it was some sort of protection.

"Hello sweet. Did you have a nice sleep?"

"What did you do to me, you bastard?" Lauren asked, staring at Max in horror.

"Don't get angry, Lauren; it's simply what you deserve."

"Deserve? What I *deserve?*! You're out of your mind, Max!"

Max stood up quickly, knocking the chair over onto its side, then stretched his hands out in front of him. His eyes wide with rage, he lunged at Lauren's throat, gripping it as tightly as he could.

Lauren heard his moans as he pressed down on her windpipe, and in between the moans, she heard his laughter. He thought this was funny. She gasped for air as her throat closed in, desperately trying to breathe as the pressure in her head began to build. There was no way she was going to be able to reason with Max, or scream for help. Her voice box felt like it was being compressed. Everything was merging into a deep, black fog. As the pressure rose in her head, sereneness calmed her and a strange, relaxed feeling swept through her body – a feeling like, maybe, she was ready to die.

It took her about thirty seconds to recognise that the pressure had been released. She blinked a few times, hearing a muffled noise, and just before everything turned black, she was sure she saw Kevin's face, staring down at her.

Chapter Twenty-eight

Kevin had finally plucked up the courage to visit Lauren in hospital; he'd left it until the third day so she'd have time to acclimatise to what she'd just been through. The bouquet in his hand was full of yellow lilies and bright pink peonies. The florist had told him the bouquet signified happiness and good fortune, and she'd also added a yellow rose for friendship for him too. The aroma wafting in front of his nose smelled divine, leaving the stench of the sterile antiseptic in the corridor behind him. He didn't want to put pressure on Lauren and possibly ruin everything with her, but if they could be friends, it would be a start.

He hadn't been able to shake his feelings for her away; he just couldn't stop thinking about her. He remembered her large hazel eyes, which only days ago had been transfixed on his, seeking out his trust – and her brown matted hair contouring her dirt-ingrained face, her beauty still shining through. She'd been so vulnerable in the crawl space when she'd suffered the panic attack that all he'd really wanted to do was cradle her in his arms, though of course he couldn't. He had to see her suffer until her breathing had become controlled. This woman was made of strong grit and determination.

He expected more traffic in the hospital… people coming and going, doctors, nurses and orderlies rushing around, even people pushing a food trolley or machinery somewhere, but there was hardly anyone walking the halls. It felt odd.

Kevin found there were a large number of rooms to the left and right of him, all of them numbered. A nurse sat at a cream wooden desk, her head down, and he walked past, not wanting to wake her. When he got to room 36, he stopped. This was the one.

His hands became clammy as he thought about what he was going to do, and just as he was about to tap on the door he heard Lauren scream, "…deserve?! You're out of your mind, Max!"

Throwing the bouquet to the floor, Kevin turned the door handle and let himself in, amazed at the sight in front of him. Without even thinking he pounced on Max, pulling at his shirt in an attempt to drag him away from Lauren. When that didn't work he moved in closer to grip him by the shoulders, pushing him backwards as he swept his own leg around Max's ankle, forcing him to the floor.

After turning over to forward roll himself back into position, Max was soon back up on his feet, and he charged at Kevin with rage in his eyes.

Kevin was too quick for him. He tensed as his neck drove his forehead into the middle of Max's face, causing blood to spatter to the ground as the bedside cabinet went sprawling over onto its side. Max, however, wasn't about to give up: he came back at Kevin with a violent blow to his temple. It stunned Kevin for a moment; Max drew breath as he threw several more punches.

The sudden smell of sweat occupied Kevin's nostrils as he realised he was backed into a corner –not a good place to be. His clenched fists met the centre of Max's face, his nose opening up even more as the blood oozed out. Still Max fought back, Kevin suffering blow after blow from a heavy fist smacking against his ribs, weakening him further.

Reaching out, Kevin yanked at the curtains, forcing the wooden pole to escape its fixings and crash down to the floor. Almost blindly, he stooped down to retrieve it as Max started kicking him repeatedly in the stomach. They struggled as the fists kept flying. Then, with one fell swoop Kevin latched onto the pole, and with a mammoth effort he smashed the piece of wood straight down the centre of Max's head.

Max fell to the ground as blood gushed from his open wound.

For a second Kevin didn't move as his eyes stayed on Max, lying there with his arms sprawled out by his sides. Stepping over him, Kevin rushed as fast as his legs would let him to Lauren's bed, immediately pressing the emergency button. He cupped Lauren's face in his hands. "Lauren, please wake up. Come on." He began to gently shake her shoulders to at least get some reaction. There was no response.

"Where are the bloody nurses?!" he shouted.

He didn't want to leave Lauren in the room – surely the horrifying image of Max swathed in blood on the hospital room floor would terrorise her – but he had no choice. He dashed to the door, his eyes fixating on Max for a brief second. He needed help as much as Lauren did, but Lauren came first. Sprinting into the corridor, he shouted for help, quickly gaining the attention of two doctors assisting a nurse – the very same nurse he'd seen earlier, slumped over her desk.

"I need help, come quickly!" he pleaded. "You need to call the police too!"

He was followed back into the room by the two male doctors, and as they quickly assessed the room one ran to Lauren's aid, the other to Max's. The doctor left Max's side to run and press the emergency button, and soon the room was filled with men and women in white coats, all rushing around with machines and other equipment. Max was put on a stretcher as a doctor compressed a white muslin cloth to the top of his head, then they rushed him out of the room.

As Lauren began to stir, she realised she was being monitored by a young nurse who was sympathetically smoothing her hand. All Kevin could do was be a bystander. He'd been told to seek medical attention himself, but he'd chosen not to; he wanted to make sure Lauren was okay.

The nurse helped Lauren sit up, and as soon as her face fell on Kevin's, tears escaped her eyes.

"Hey beautiful. How you doing?" Kevin asked.

"Me? Look at you! What happened?" Lauren's eyes widened as flashes of memories started coming back to her. "Max was here! Where is he now?"

Kevin could see the terror in her eyes, and not for the first time, he silently cursed Max Davies.

"It's okay, he's in theatre," said the nurse.

Kevin looked at her in astonishment. Max was alive? How could that be? He'd been dead, he was sure of it.

"In theatre, but why?" asked Kevin.

"He's fighting for his life," the nurse replied before adding, "I'm Joanna, I'll be looking after Lauren."

"Will he live?" asked Lauren.

"We don't know. Can you remember anything, Lauren?" Joanna frowned, clearly concerned.

"It's a blur, but yes I remember he was here. Kevin, though... I don't remember you being here. Wait! I remember seeing your face as everything turned black. He put me to sleep, what was he going to do?"

"Lauren, you need to rest, you must calm yourself," Joanna told her, noticing her excessive involuntary movements. She was concerned about the side effects of the Propofol; Lauren would have to be closely monitored for days. The nurse also noticed that Lauren's mouth was beginning to water – hypersalivation was another side effect of Propofol. "I think it would be best if you did get yourself seen to, Kevin," Joanna told him. "I'll arrange for Lauren to be moved to a different room. This is now a crime scene."

"No, I don't want him to leave!" shouted Lauren, panicking.

Kevin walked over and took her hand, kissing the back of her palm softly. She looked so vulnerable, just like when she'd emerged from the crawl space. *How much more could this young lady take?* he thought. "Don't worry, I'll be right here," he told her. "I'm not leaving this building without you. You need to listen to the experts, Lauren, so you can recover."

"Mr Williams," a uniformed police officer said as he entered the room, "we need to ask you some questions."

"Sure," replied Kevin.

"Could we go somewhere a little more private?" the policeman asked. "Ms Adams, when you're feeling well enough I'd like to ask you a few questions too."

The man's soft face encouraged Lauren to relax slightly. She nodded.

"I'll be right back, Lauren," Kevin told her, kissing her hand again.

He followed the officer out into the corridor. It was a scene of activity, nothing like the eeriness of when he'd first stepped into the building. "How is Max Davies doing, officer?" he asked sternly.

"Inspector Nolan." He held his hand out to shake Kevin's hand. "I haven't had an update, but last I heard he was in a life-threatening condition." Kevin looked down at the ground. "There's a room here we can go into, get all the questions out the way. Then you can return to Ms Adams."

Once they were inside the room, Inspector Nolan motioned his hand towards the chair, gesturing for Kevin to sit down. Kevin sat, listening to what the inspector had to say. It appeared the police were well aware of Max Davies's backstory. He'd eluded them many times. They still had a job to do, though: to work out what had happened in the hospital room.

Kevin gave his account of what happened, and it didn't take long for Inspector Nolan to let him go. He'd need to make a formal statement at some point, but for now he could return to Lauren.

In the meantime, Lauren had been moved to another room, and before going in Kevin paused anxiously outside. He didn't know what he was going to tell her. Max was still alive, but in a critical condition. Should he tell her now or give her time to recover? Either way, he was sure her reaction would be one of disbelief.

"Kevin, how are you?" When she saw him, Lauren immediately raised herself up on the bed, resting her head against two plumped up pillows. She smiled at him brightly, though she still looked very weak.

"Don't worry about me, how are you doing?"

Lauren shook her head. "I was just lying here, wondering when all this was going to end. What's happening with Max?"

Kevin hesitated for a moment, then told her, "He's in a critical condition, but he made it through surgery."

Lauren's face fell. "I need to get out of here, Kevin – I don't want to be anywhere near him. I'm scared."

Kevin nodded. "I'll see what I can do, but if you're not allowed to leave then I'll stay with you. I won't let anything happen to you, Lauren." He sat down on the edge of the bed, picked up Lauren's hand, and held it gently.

Lauren found that she quite liked him doing this – the first time she thought he'd done it just as friends, but now, it seemed like it meant something different.

"Is there anything you need?" he asked softly.

"All I need is to leave this place."

Kevin jumped up from the bed. "I won't be long, I promise."

As she watched him walk out the door, Lauren felt immediately vulnerable. She hated being alone.

Kevin went straight to speak to Joanna, telling her it was in Lauren's best interest for her to be released from hospital. Her mental health was deteriorating, and she was terrified of being in the same building as Max.

"Okay," Joanna agreed, "but someone needs to be with her, to stay with her and monitor her."

"I'll take care of her," Kevin vowed, "I promise."

"And you'll have to return in the morning for Lauren to have further assessments," Joanna continued.

"Tomorrow morning. Got it."

Lauren happily agreed to Kevin's offer – she'd be only too glad of his company, and she would be safe away from Max, even though she knew he was on his deathbed. She still couldn't shake her feelings of terror, imagining he could still get to her, but the thought of being at the top of a high building gave her some confidence – Kevin lived in a penthouse suite.

She looked around the suite in appreciation. She didn't quite know what she'd been expecting, but she liked what she saw. It was homely and cosy, the luxury features of the open-plan dining room being filled with modern charm. A Venetian mirror surmounted the mantel. In her bedroom for the night, ornate silver bedside tables – with matching table lamps – flanked the bespoke bed. Some black and red damask wall coverings made the room nice and vibrant, while white silk sheets gave the room a touch of class. The en-suite bathroom, which was decorated with black and white marble tiles, gleamed; the bath and shower looked like they'd never been used.

That made Lauren think: had Kevin ever had a wife? She didn't know much about him, yet here she was in his fabulous home. Thinking about it, he was almost a stranger. When would she ever learn?

Suddenly she became panicked, the muscle jerking returning. A tap on the door startled her.

"You okay in there?" shouted Kevin.

"Come in," replied Lauren.

Kevin entered with a big beam on his face. "I hope you have everything you need."

"Umm – yes, thanks, but… well… I don't think it's a good idea I stay here, now that I think about it. I'm going to ring Jacob to pick me up. I hope you don't mind."

Kevin's smile faded. "If that's what you want, Lauren, then of course. But why?"

Her eyes watered as she stared at Kevin. "I got close to a stranger once before and look what happened."

His features softened. "I'm not Max."

"I know – you saved me, and I will always be grateful for that. It's going to take me a long time to trust someone again, that's all."

"I understand. You're shaking. Look, you need to rest; I was under strict instructions to look after you, and that's what I want to do." He took a step closer. "Lauren, I don't know everything you've been through, but I am here to help. I promise."

Lauren smiled, and as she looked into Kevin's eyes, she knew she could trust him. He wasn't Max and he never would be. "Okay, I'll stay. Thank you."

Kevin's smile came back then. "Great! I'll make you some supper – you need to eat. Make yourself comfortable, and if you need anything just give me a shout." He gave her a wink as he left the room, heading for the kitchen.

Lauren sat on the bed, thinking for a moment. She *did* feel safe here. Smiling, she slipped in between the silk sheets and as her head hit the pillow, she was gone.

*****

As the morning light lit up the room, Lauren shuddered for a second as she wondered where she was.

Sitting up, she looked around her, relief flooding through her entire body as she recognised the bedroom. She was still in a safe place, and not only that – she was feeling so much better. The spasms had completely ceased.

She knew she needed to go to the hospital and get checked over, but she didn't want to leave. It was like she had – finally – escaped and ended up somewhere far away, secluded from everything that had happened. She wanted it to stay like this, but she knew it wasn't reality.

There was one thing she had to do before she could move on. And today she felt strong enough to do it.

Chapter Twenty-nine

As Kevin parked the car, Lauren looked up at the hospital building. To her it looked sombre and ominous. It wasn't a place she wanted to re-enter, but she'd made a promise to herself and she was going to see it through.

"Are you sure you want me to wait here?" asked Kevin.

"Yes, I won't be long. It's just a check-up."

He smiled. "I'll be waiting for you."

Lauren climbed out of the car and gave a wave as she walked towards the building, taking a deep breath as she entered through the doors. The smell of antiseptic made her flinch back. Trying to keep calm, she took long strides to reach reception, where a young spectacled male was perched behind the desk.

"Excuse me, I'm here to visit Max Davies. Can you tell me what room he's in?"

"Just a moment, let me check. Are you a relative?"

"Yes, I'm his sister," Lauren lied.

The receptionist frowned as he looked at his computer screen. "I'm sorry, but your brother is still in intensive care – he had a bad night."

"Oh no, I need to see him!" Lauren began to cry. The young man handed her a tissue. "Thank you."

"I'm sorry, madam," he said, looking genuinely upset. He picked up the phone and rang through to the ICU, discussing the matter with whoever was on the other end. "They'll let you in to see him but you won't be able to stay long."

"Thank you."

"Take the lift to level three – turn right, follow the arrows, and it will take you to the ICU."

"Thank you, again."

Lauren followed his directions, and when she got there she peered into Max's room through the window. He was linked up to several machines, not much of his skin showing. A bandage was covering his scalp. Heading inside, she pulled up a chair next to his bed, staring at him long and hard. How vulnerable he looked now!

"How does it feel, Max?" she asked, venom in her voice. "On your deathbed? You can't touch me now. You tried to break me, and you failed. You tried to kill me, and you failed. In the end, you simply couldn't get rid of me; *I was too strong for you.* You haven't destroyed me, and you never will."

She paused for a moment, trying to keep her emotions in check. She didn't want to alert any of the doctors or nurses. Not yet.

"I admit, you took part of my life away when you killed my mother…" She paused again, her voice catching in her throat as she thought of her poor mum, racing in to save her children only to be met with death herself. "And for that," she continued, her voice slightly shakier now, "I can never, ever forgive you." She took a deep breath, wiping a tear from her eye before continuing. "But I am *not* going to waste my time and energy thinking about you and what you did. I still have a life to live, which is more than can be said for you." She laughed, a laugh full of bitterness and hatred. "Do you hear me, Max? You haven't broken me; you've only made me stronger."

Lauren stared at his face, and for a brief moment she thought she saw his eyes flicker. Did it actually happen or was it just wishful thinking, hoping he could hear her as she spoke of his impending death?

No, she didn't imagine it – there it was again: a slight movement of the eye. He could hear her, she was sure of it.

"I know you can hear me, Max. I know you can tell what I'm saying, and I'm glad." She took another deep breath, pasting a smile on her face as she finished, "The last word I will ever say to you is: Goodbye."

She knew she'd won, and as she left she felt as if some of the tension was lifted from her shoulders. This was the end – the end of the nightmare that had begun with that monster, lying there immobilised and broken.

She turned around for one last look at him as the noise of the machines started to buzz and ring. Quickly getting out of the way, she watched from the corridor as doctors and nurses made a frantic rush to his bedside. The emergency crash team were trying to revive him, and though CPR wasn't working, they kept on trying. And trying. And trying. It was no use.

With a smile on her face, Lauren walked away as the long, slow beep told her Max was dead.

Billy

All his life Billy had lived in an establishment that catered for his special needs, and at least twice a year Max would visit him and take him out on a day trip. Billy had always loved the time he spent with Max, though he never really understood why he couldn't live with him or see him more regularly. Twin brothers were supposed to be together all the time, weren't they? Best friends who have double the fun!

On this particular day Billy wondered why he was made to go to Max's house and remain upstairs in a small room. They usually did things like going to the park or the bowling alley, or at least some sort of activity. He'd been happy to see Max, but he was bored today.

Max brought him lunch and a puzzle of the Eiffel Tower to complete, which he'd started working on straight away, smiling as he saw the top of the tower staring back at him. He loved tall buildings and structures, and he loved puzzles, but this one took him hours to complete.

When darkness fell Billy heard raised voices, and suddenly his room lit up, flashes of blue and orange everywhere. There was a strange smell too, like when he went to the petrol station with Max to fill up the car to make it go faster. He hated that smell; it played havoc with his senses.

The door to the room was locked, so – as usual – Billy turned it into a game. When he heard footsteps he hid until Max could find him. Max wasn't talking clearly, and he seemed strange. Billy had trouble understanding him, and every now and again water ran down Max's cheek.

The loud noise outside was keeping him awake. He looked through the slit in the curtains, scared to open them any wider. There were men dressed in black trousers and shirts, all looking the same. Someone was holding a large trumpet to their mouth, words running out of it like a concertina.

Max was shouting again, and suddenly Billy became very frightened. He wanted to leave, to go back to Maggie. She would give him tea and biscuits. He didn't like today – it wasn't as much fun as usual.

He tried the handle to the door, glad to find that Max hadn't shut him in, after all. Clearly, Max had started a new game. Tiptoeing out of the bedroom, Billy crept along the landing, quiet as a mouse. He placed his finger over his mouth, reminding himself to remain silent. He didn't want Max to find him yet.

The flashing lights were there again, lighting up the hall. Ignoring them, Billy continued to inch his way into the kitchen. There was darkness everywhere. A deep thudding noise made him jump and turn around – he'd always hated loud noises.

As a young boy – before he was taken to Maggie's – he could always remember his mother shouting at Max. He used to cover his ears with his hands to block it out. His mother had loved Billy dearly; he would sit on his mother's lap and she would rock him back and forth. She never did this with Max. When she died in the fire he went to a much more peaceful place. No more loud noises, no more things being smashed up... it was a place he called home. Max didn't go with him, though – he went away on his own. At first Billy had felt lonely, but as he settled in he became friends with people just like him.

Slowly, Billy neared the basement – it was so dark, except for a torch light. A large piece of carpet was lying at the foot of the steps. An arm with mottled brown marks on its skin was poking out the side, red paint staining the fingers.

"What the hell are you doing here?" asked Max as he pushed Billy back into the kitchen.

"I heard noises. I don't like noises. Who was that on the steps? Why is there red paint on their fingers?"

"Never you mind about that," snarled Max.

"What is that smell, Max? Why are there people outside dressed in black and shouting through a trumpet?"

"What's with all the questions?" Max ushered him into the dining room.

"No, it smells."

"Sit there and don't move. You hear me?"

Billy sat with his hands pressed in his lap. He wondered why Max wasn't talking properly. He began to feel agitated. This was not what they usually did. What was wrong?

A bright light illuminated the room then, a sudden noise deafening him. He was tossed into the air like a rag doll, landing heavily on his head.

He woke to incredible shock – it reminded him of the time he had once dived into a freezing cold sea. His breath was slowly ebbing away from him, and he couldn't focus on his bearings. The pain was beyond anything he'd ever felt before. He was experiencing his body doing a thousand crazy things. His legs had been flayed off from the bone and a burning sensation was running through him. His brain was scrambled and he knew he couldn't stay conscious much longer. His breathing was noisy, like a child's rattle when they shake it, his beating heart struggling. Sinking into unconsciousness, he felt very cool and relaxed. There was no need to breathe anymore. He wasn't scared now – not now there was no pain of any kind, totally peaceful.

Everything grew dark around the edges until his eyes slowly closed.

Chapter Thirty

Lauren, Jacob, and Kevin all sat together, waiting for Inspector Mann to begin. He'd urgently called them together to tell them some important news.

"Max had been living a double life," the inspector told them. "He'd fabricated his role of Mr Reynolds, a teacher in Salford Primary. He did it to get close to you, Lauren. He'd overheard you talking about the planned weekend away with your friends to Butlin's holiday park, and he seized the opportunity to get to know you. He'd arranged for Thomas Victor to meet him that night in the grounds. Thomas Victor had refused Max's offer of committing fraud – just like you, Jacob – so he killed him."

Jacob nodded. He didn't want to interrupt the inspector.

"Max needed to get rid of Victor quickly. His plot wasn't foolproof, and yet somehow everything went according to plan. He'd even fooled the court by getting acquitted. The arrangement of his vendetta against Jacob was a cruel act of surreal revenge; he even sacrificed his twin brother in order to achieve his obsession. His past history has links to other fraudulent acts, overseas." Inspector Mann sighed, shaking his head. "I have to say, this case has been the most harrowing and unbelievable I've ever witnessed in my thirty-year career in the police force. I want you to promise me, Lauren, that Max Davies won't take any more of your life away. He died of an injury inflicted by an innocent party. Kevin, you will not be punished in any way. Max Davies hid his murderous trail with deceit and lies. I wish you well, Lauren," he finished, with real empathy in his voice. By now the inspector felt an emotional bond with Lauren, and he knew he would never forget her.

Lauren sat open-mouthed as she listened. Kevin was by her side, as he had been ever since he'd rescued her. She was still living at his penthouse. She didn't want to be alone – not just yet. She couldn't quite take in what Inspector Mann had just said, of how Max had gone to such extreme lengths to get back at Jacob. He'd tortured her, killed her beloved mum, murdered an innocent man, and even killed his twin brother. She couldn't believe it.

"I won't let him ruin any more of my life, Inspector," she said, her voice loud and confident, "you can count on that."

*****

Lauren sat attentively, eyeing the decor. This was a big step for her. Natural light was shining through the bay window, subdued yet coordinated colours adding warmth and openness. Pleasant artwork matched the patterned ornaments dotted about the place. The ambience couldn't help but relax her.

In adjusting to life after being held hostage, Lauren was experiencing typical stress reactions, intrusive thoughts often leading her back to her time as a victim. Denial, impaired memory, and decreased concentration all contributed to the fear of it happening again. The physical torture she went through – the long periods of isolation and the physical abuse – were being addressed by the medical team. Going through the debrief process had had a therapeutic effect on Lauren, and she recognised this as the start of her reintegration. Experiencing sleep disturbance, flashbacks, and nightmares made her feel even angrier towards Max.

Carol Cato reminded her on a daily basis that this was a completely normal reaction; it would not only take her body time to recover, but also her mind. Carol was an experienced member of the medical team, her warm nature equalling her warm brown eyes. She reminded Lauren that the withdrawal and avoidance of family, friends, and activities – as well as the constant feeling of being on edge – was normal.

"Such reactions to an extremely stressful event are understandable, Lauren. These are typical responses and generally decrease after a period of time, so try not to worry. In terms of healing from the psychological strain of being a kidnap victim, it is necessary for you to undergo cognitive behavioural therapy so you can permanently recover."

"I'm going to do everything you suggest," Lauren replied.

"This will involve you changing your way of thinking, Lauren, replacing negatives with positives. An event such as a kidnapping can cause very deep negative connections, and these connections need to be rewired in order to reach a point of normality once again."

Lauren nodded, hanging on Carol's every word.

"This psychological debriefing is a preventive measure to help reduce the psychological effects of your kidnapping," Carol continued. "You will undergo a series of meetings that will allow you to confront the kidnapping, torture, and bereavement you've endured. You will also be able to share your feelings with a counsellor to help structure your memories. All these therapies will help you, Lauren, if you give them a good try."

Carol smiled and Lauren relaxed. She hadn't spoken much in this session, just listened.

"Rebuilding your life is going to take time, but being patient and kind to yourself will enable you to eventually come to terms with your ordeal. Establishing routine into your everyday life is a must. If you go to the shops, take a walk, and try to do it every day. This will help to erase the routines you were set by your perpetrator." Carol didn't want to use the name Max Davies; that name, she said, should be eradicated from Lauren Adams' mind.

Lauren thought long and hard, her eyes still transfixed on the lovely lady sitting opposite her. She realised life was becoming easier for her, but she knew she still had a long way to go.

She also knew that she *would* get there. After all, she'd already taken a huge step by being present at this meeting – the first step of many.

*****

For six months now Lauren had been healing, and the support from Jacob and her friends had been amazing, but they didn't really know what she'd been through and sometimes she sensed that they didn't know what to say to her. But here she was, standing on the doorstep and ready to swipe her ID card to walk through the automatic door. For a moment she turned her head and looked up into the sky. It was a beautiful morning, the sky's orange hue indicating the possibility of a sunny day.

She smiled. Making the major decision to return to work felt good. It would be a new beginning, the beginning of her new life.

*****

Epilogue

Lauren was healing well. Although she knew she'd never be the same person as she was before her captivity, she'd already learnt several coping strategies to manage the tough days that still inevitably intruded upon her. At least since her return to Salford Primary, normality had begun to creep in; working from eight until four with young children didn't give her much time to think about anything else.

It was the end of another working week and Lauren was waiting for Jacob; they met every Friday afternoon in the café around the corner from Salford Primary. One of the only good things to come out of all this was the time she got to spend with her brother, who'd decided to stay in England. It was good having him so close. After years of him living in Canada, she knew she could now rely on Jacob to be there in a flash if she needed him.

When he walked through the door, she looked up and smiled. Wearing a charcoal slim fit suit, azure blue shirt, and black tie – with his converse man bag thrown over his shoulder – he really looked the part. A typical yuppie. His transfer from Fairfax Financial to a respectable recruitment agency in Manchester suited him, his managerial skills having taken him to new heights. He was settled here again, rebuilding his life as best he could. Lauren knew he was still full of guilt and that he was trying his hardest to put things right, and she loved him for it.

"Hi Sis, your usual?" Jacob asked as he kissed her on the cheek.

"Yes please."

Lauren watched as he ordered their lattes. He was the only family she had now; although her friendship group was a kind of family to her, they weren't blood relatives. Max Davies had stolen that from her.

Lauren could speak of Max now without the seething anger she used to feel when she mentioned his name, but the steps he took to seek revenge on Jacob and destroy their lives were never going to go away.

Kevin was the other good thing to resurrect itself from the traumatic event Max had inflicted upon her; Lauren's face lit up whenever she thought of him. He was her saviour, literally, saving her from the depths of despair when he'd rescued her, and continuing to save her every day since – even now.

Living together in his penthouse, they were beginning their future together, a future she never thought she would have.

Smiling, she rubbed her hand over her stomach – she couldn't wait to meet this little one.

THE END

ABOUT THE AUTHOR

Ruth O'Neill grew up in the city of Bath, England. She has always enjoyed helping others and is very committed to her job as a Teaching Assistant for Literacy. Employed by the Cabot Learning Federation, she works in one of their community schools The City Academy Bristol, where she supports young people with Special Educational Needs & Disabilities. She has lived in the city of Bristol for thirty-five years.

Ruth is a member of the writing community on twitter where you can follow her at https://twitter.com/ruthoneill1 where there will be an announcement on her fourth book ULTIMATE BETRAYAL next year.

L - #0629 - 021219 - C0 - 210/148/12 - PB - DID2695418